THE
WAY STATION
GAMBIT

PART TWO OF THE
CONTINGENCY WAR SERIES

G J OGDEN

ISBN-13: 978-1-9160426-4-3

Cover design by germancreative
Editing by S L Ogden

www.ogdenmedia.net

THE CONTINGENCY WAR SERIES

No-one comes in peace. Every being in the galaxy wants something, and is willing to take it by force...

READ THE OTHER BOOKS IN THE SERIES:

- The Contingency
- The Way Station Gambit
- Rise of Nimrod Fleet
- Earth's Last War

ACKNOWLEDGEMENTS

Thanks to Sarah for her work assessing and editing this novel, and to those who subscribed to my newsletters and provided such valuable feedback.

And thanks, as always, to anyone who is reading this. It means a lot. If you enjoyed it, please help by leaving a review on Amazon and Goodreads to let other potential readers know what you think!

If you'd like updates on future novels by G J Ogden, please consider subscribing to the mailing list. Your details will be used to notify subscribers about upcoming books from this author, in addition to a hand-selected mix of book offers and giveaways from similar SFF authors.

http://subscribe.ogdenmedia.net

ONE

A deep, resonant tone pulsed through the bridge of the Hedalt War Frigate and the light level dropped to a dark crimson hue, changing the steel-gray complexion of Provost Adra to a blood red. She lifted her head, her tight, black ponytail brushing down the back of her armored uniform, and studied the halo of screens encircling the command platform. She was adept at selecting only the most pertinent items of data, and soon her eyes fell on the cause of the automatic switch to battle conditions; three contacts had jumped into the system, still distant, but closing on her position fast.

Adjutant Lux raced back to his station between the twin pilot simulants at the front of the bridge, beneath the giant viewport that spread out above him in a wide arc. He read the information on his console and then turned to address Provost Adra. "Three contacts. None are transmitting valid transceiver signals. All three are on an intercept course."

"Racketeers," said Adra, spitting out the word as if it were a rotten fruit. She quickly assessed the scan information on the approaching ships, all of which appeared to be equipped with black-market transceivers to hide their identities and allow them to travel through the Fabric without being monitored. The lead ship was an old Corvette-class cruiser, which had likely been stolen from a breaking yard. Nearly all of this class of ship, with the exception of a handful of remaining Hunter Corvettes, had been mothballed decades or longer ago. The other two racketeer vessels were light freighters that had been heavily modified with weapons and armor. Even together, the trio of pirates posed little threat to Adra's powerful War Frigate, but Adra's vessel was not the target. Their plan was to raid the freighters that she was escorting; a tedious duty, but one she accepted as a necessary part of her role. The cargo that these particular freighters contained – jump fuel, medicines, food and more – were extremely valuable, both to the Hedalt Empire and to the colonies that inhabited the titanic Way Stations. The city-sized space stations had been left by the mysterious race that had once enslaved the Hedalt, and who they had eventually rebelled against and overthrown. Purged of their former owners, the Way Stations were now Hedalt cities scattered among the stars, many of which were located in the fringe regions, beyond the watch or care of the empire.

The racketeers' main tactic was to draw away any defensive escort and then disable a single freighter, knowing that the standard order for Warfare Command vessels such as Adra's frigate was to remain with and defend the surviving ships. The disabled freighter would then fall behind and become easy pickings for the racketeers. But Adra knew these tactics well; in fact she was counting on the predictability and linear thinking of the pirates, whose lesser minds and petty thievery Adra despised.

"Signal our escorts that we are moving to engage the racketeers, and order them to continue on course. They are not to deviate, under any circumstances."

"Yes, Provost," Lux replied, but then hesitantly added, "but should we not instruct the escorts to change course away from the racketeer vessels?"

"I gave you a command, Adjutant," snapped Adra, "Now carry it out."

Lux nodded humbly and turned, knocking the primary pilot simulant on the shoulder with the back of his hand; it responded by changing course and accelerating hard towards the oncoming ships. Lux then relayed Adra's command to the lead ship of their four freighter escorts, and enabled the tactical layout on the main viewport. The image switched to show a zoomed-in view of the three attacking vessels.

Adra pointed to one of the screens above her and then drew her hand towards her chest, causing the screen to swing down on a silver arm that seemed too thin to support its weight, yet did so without sign of strain. She grabbed the frame of the display and re-positioned it to her left side. On the screen was her customized tactical console, from which she would direct the attack personally. Adra preferred not to let the simulants have too much control over battle operations. Despite the tactical simulants being allowed a level of strategic intelligence, she believed their lobotomized lab-grown human brains lacked a natural feel for combat and the insight as to when and where to strike hardest.

A low tone sounded again, and Adra saw that the lead racketeer ship had launched four missiles at them. *Pitiful...* thought Adra, countering with a spread of decoy drones, which shot out ahead of the frigate to intercept the missiles. Seconds later, four bright flashes lit up the viewport as the missiles detonated harmlessly in space.

"The two smaller racketeer ships are breaking off to pursue the freighters," Lux called out, though this was exactly as Adra had already predicted. "The lead Corvette is reducing velocity, but it remains on an intercept course with us."

"Its plan is to lure us away," Adra replied, coolly. "Adjust course to pursue the two breakaway ships, and reduce our velocity just enough to allow the lead Corvette to close."

Unseen by Adra, Lux raised his eyebrows, surprised that the Provost would allow the enemy ship within weapons range, while also allowing the other two ships to get further ahead. The Corvette may have been old, but it still possessed sufficient firepower to cripple or even destroy a War Frigate if allowed to advance unchallenged. But, still smarting from being reproached earlier, he chose not to query the command and simply relayed the orders to the appropriate members of their mostly simulant crew. Nevertheless, the tiny hesitation that occurred between Adra's order and its execution had not gone unnoticed by the Provost.

The bridge shook as cannon fire from the pursuing Corvette hammered into the rear ablative hull plating, which bore the impact without any resulting damage to the frigate's systems. Adra watched the pursuing ship closely on her screen, while frequently flicking her intense blue eyes to the main viewport in order to keep tabs on the other two racketeers. The Corvette continued to close, seemingly gaining in confidence, and the War Frigate was pounded again, but this time warnings flashed up on Adra's screen, indicating that the barrage had broken through their thick armor, causing minor damage. She glanced around the side of her screen to check on Lux, watching with interest to see whether her inexperienced new adjutant was managing to keep his composure. Lux had grasped hold of the metal frames of the two pilot's chairs to either side, holding them as one would if going over the dip of a rollercoaster. *At least he had the sense to keep his mouth shut this time*, Adra mused.

The pursuing Corvette continued to close and Adra smiled as the distance indicator finally dropped to the number she was waiting for. *Greed and stupidity are common partners,* she thought, and then she pressed a single button on her console screen to execute her pre-planned maneuver. The thrusters fired, spinning the mighty frigate a full one hundred and eighty degrees and then shunting it laterally, while keeping the main forward plasma cannons carefully trained on the Corvette. She watched patiently as the ship desperately tried to turn away, but the crew knew, as did Adra, that their exuberance had cost them dearly. She tried to imagine the scenes of panic on the bridge; the cries of terror, the shouts of blame, as each turned on the other. There was no honor on a racketeer ship. She was doing them a favor by reducing their archaic little vessel to atoms.

Adra waited until the last moment, allowing them a few more moments of agony, and perhaps even a glimmer of hope – a belief that they might yet get away, that they might still live – and then she fired. Three twin pulses of searing purple energy erupted towards the racketeer ship, each striking the hull cleanly and scorching deep furrows into its heart. Moments later the Corvette was consumed by light and blown apart into thousands of pieces. Adra spun the ship back around and pushed the main engines twenty percent beyond maximum, entering her command override to dismiss the warning that flashed up, cautioning her of possible engine damage.

"Bring us within weapons range of the two remaining ships," Adra called out to Lux, who had now released his vice-like grip on the pilot's chair. To Adra's satisfaction, he responded without hesitation, and relayed the commands. The beat of the War Frigate's engines through the deck plating caused the entire bridge to vibrate as if subjected to powerful seismic waves, as the mighty vessel cut through space like a shark tearing through the ocean in pursuit of prey.

"One of the two remaining racketeer ships has

abandoned the pursuit," Lux called back, raising his voice to a near shout to be heard over the drone of the engines. "It is heading away on a perpendicular course."

Adra watched the ship peel away and start to run. She could practically smell the fear of the crew on-board, and it only spurred her on harder. She knew they would have witnessed the destruction of their leader and realized that they were next, and like their comrades, they would now foolishly cling to the hope they might survive. But by changing course they had in fact allowed Adra to gain on them more rapidly. She selected the ship on her panel and launched three torpedoes, watching on the main viewport as the weapons streaked towards their target. She relished the thought of the doomed racketeers helplessly watching the torpedoes approach, and suffering the gut-wrenching realization that there was nothing they could do to prevent their deaths. A flash of orange and red lit up the viewport and the ship blinked and disappeared from Adra's screen.

Suddenly, the angry pulse of the engines decreased and Adra glanced at her console, noting that the ship was decelerating rapidly. Furious, she shoved away her screen, ready to challenge Lux and to demand an explanation, when the reason became obvious; the final racketeer had halted its pursuit of the freighters and was signaling its surrender.

"We are receiving a communication request from the remaining racketeer," said Lux. "They wish to surrender and submit to judgment by Warfare Command, without preconditions."

Adra laughed, but it was a mocking laugh; one that conveyed no joy, only derision. "Without preconditions," she said, repeating Lux's words. "They offer this as if they have a choice".

The frigate came to a stop one hundred meters in front of the dilapidated and battle-scarred light freighter, which was less than a quarter of its size. Adra scanned the vessel, noting that its jump drive was not charged and that its meagre weapon systems had been deactivated. She targeted the bridge of the ship with the dorsal nose turret and then accepted the communication request. A second later the terrified face of the racketeer captain appeared on the viewport. He was small for a Hedalt, thin and with messy, knotted hair pressed underneath a black headscarf. Guilt was inscribed across his face like scars.

Adra despised this element of her race; the criminal underworld that had grown up as the Hedalt had expanded through space, feeding off the weak and vulnerable inhabitants of the Way Stations like vermin. They were little better than humans to Adra. This captain, at least, had more gumption than his companions, because he knew the law that guaranteed a hearing to any Hedalt subject who submits freely. But Adra did not care for this particular law, and as a military provost, she had the authority to serve as judge, jury and, if she desired, executioner.

"Provost, we surrender freely," said the racketeer captain, his voice crackly and unsure. "We have powered down our weapons and jump engines and await boarding."

Adra shook her head. There was no humility in the request, just an implied understanding that Adra would abide by the law. They knew that by surrendering and submitting to tribunal they would at least be spared death, and so they did so only to save their skins. *Cowards...* Adra thought.

"Apologize," said Adra, fixing the racketeer with a unwavering stare.

The racketeer captain looked confused, and glanced off to the side, presumably to look at one or more of his other crewmates. "I don't understand, Provost."

"Apologize," Adra repeated. "Apologize for your pathetic attempt to raid this convoy. Apologize for the disgrace that you are to the Hedaltus race. Apologize for wasting my time."

This appeared to anger the racketeer leader, and even embolden him. "I and my crew have a right to trial. I do not need to apologize to you,

Provost. You are obliged to do your duty!"

"This is your trial," spat Adra, "and this is your sentence." She practically punched the screen to her side, causing the forward turret to unleash a hail-storm of needle-like plasma shards into the bridge of the racketeer ship. Adra watched the viewport with satisfaction as the strips of energy tore through the Captain's torso, arms and neck, and ripped apart the consoles in the background of the image, until the image itself fizzled and went blank, to be replaced a moment later by a view of the light freighter, venting atmosphere through the gaping holes in the hull that used to surround its command center.

Lux turned to face Adra, concentrating hard in order to conceal his shock at what he'd just witnessed. This was not the first time he had seen Adra act unilaterally with deadly force, but the manner of this execution was even more sadistic than the last time she had ruthlessly eliminated a racketeer crew. He watched and waited as his commander casually waved her screen away, sending it back up to join the halo of other screens above her head.

"Do you have something to say, Adjutant Lux?" Adra asked, watching Lux closely; studying his body language and the subtle twitches of his facial muscles. The young adjutant was clearly deeply conflicted about what she had just done, but Adra was keen to learn if he was foolish enough to question her decision.

"Only that I have initiated repairs and that Warfare Command has relayed instructions for our next escort duty," Lux answered. "Shall I set a course?"

"No, I have already relayed to you our next set of co-ordinates," said Adra, pleased that Lux had sense enough not to voice any objection. "Once the freighters have passed inside the safe perimeter of the Way Station, jump at once."

Lux turned to check the co-ordinates Adra had sent over, and frowned. They indicated a position far out towards the galactic center, thousands of light years from where Warfare Command had ordered them to proceed. He turned back to Adra and tried to phrase his question without sounding rebellious. Directly challenging the order of a superior could often be a fatal mistake.

"Provost, this location is a significant distance from the co-ordinates that Warfare Command transmitted. I merely ask for clarification, in order to confirm these co-ordinates are correct."

"They are correct," Adra replied instantly, but she could see from Lux's pained expression that this answer had not allayed his confusion. For the sake of expedience, she decided to explain further, in the hope it would discourage further questions. "We are to investigate the origin of the signal anomaly that we detected in the CoreNet."

This didn't tally with the orders Lux had seen, and curiosity got the better of him, "Of course, Provost. Has Warfare Command requested we investigate the anomaly further?"

"As far as you are concerned, I *am* Warfare Command," Adra replied, glowering at him. "I grow tired of your questions, Adjutant Lux – do not ask another."

A threat was implied, and Lux heard it loud and clear. He bowed, lowering his eyes to the deck. "Apologies, Provost Adra, " he answered, realizing that he had again overstepped. It was a dangerous habit and one he knew he had to temper quickly. "I will begin preparations to jump at once." He then turned to relay the order to the simulants, but as he worked he was unable to keep his eyes off the image of the little racketeer ship on the viewport, which was still bleeding atmosphere out into space. He felt a chill of fear run down his spine, not because of where they were going, but because of who was leading him there.

TWO

Captain Taylor Ray leant forward in the command chair of the Hedalt Corvette that, prior to his 'awakening' on the Contingency base, he had believed to be an Earth Fleet Nimrod-class cruiser. It was one of many deceptions the Hedalt Empire had programmed the lab-grown brain in his simulant head into believing, through a mix of neural technology and trickery.

He was staring at a super-luminal transceiver on the viewport, quietly studying it as it spun silently in space, looking like the ball of a medieval morning star. Taylor had never given a second thought to the appearance of these devices before, but it was now obvious just how alien it was. It looked alien, because it was alien, and although its true origins still remained shrouded in mystery, its purpose was well understood. Each super-luminal transceiver was connected to others through engineered wormholes called threads. Together the threads wove a patchwork quilt of navigable lanes throughout most of the galaxy, hence the name, 'the Fabric'.

The Fabric was the basis of all interstellar travel and, through a vast network called the CoreNet, it enabled faster-than-light communication and data transmission too. It was controlled by a race called the Hedalt; violent humanoid warriors, who had approached Earth under a banner of peace, but then attacked without explanation or warning. They gave no quarter, eventually nuking the planet and almost eradicating the human species entirely.

Taylor had only learned all this a few days ago, but remarkably it wasn't the most significant revelation he'd had to deal with in that period of time.

He pushed himself out of the chair and walked up behind the empty pilot's seat, resting his forearms on the backrest. *Earth...* he mused. *I wonder if I'll ever see it for real? I wonder if it will be anything like my memory of it?*

Since the Hedalt's destruction of Earth, almost all that remained of humanity were simulants. With the exception of four unique models, these were cybernetic slaves with synthetic bodies and lobotomized lab-grown human brains.

There had been debate amongst Earth's scientists over the true origin of simulant technology – some had believed that, like the super-luminal transceivers, their existence pre-dated the Hedalt Empire. But in the same way the Hedalt now controlled the Fabric, simulant tech now served the empire too.

Simulants were used to work the mines and farms and factories that drove the Hedalt Empire, but one of their key functions was to crew their ships. Something about Hedalt biology made super-luminal travel intensely painful, even life-threatening, and so only a handful of exceptional Hedalt military officers physically manned the ships of their formidable armada.

The four special cases were the simulants that crewed the Hedalt Hunter Corvettes. These were authentic cybernetic replications of four former Earth Fleet officers: Technical Specialist Satomi Rose, Pilot Casey Valera, Tactical Specialist Blake Meade and Captain Taylor Ray – himself, or at least who he used to be, before his awakening. These advanced simulants had been designed for the sole purpose of pursuing the dregs of humanity to extinction in the years after the end of the war. Programmed using advanced neural technology woven into their lab-grown brains, they believed that Earth had won the war and that they were merely scouting space for signs of their former foes. The trickery ran so deep that they were even deceived into seeing human beings as nightmarish beasts that they believed were Hedalt, to make it easier for their still-human consciences to make the kills. After all, there were no moral dilemmas when it came to killing monsters. This insidious and highly efficient ruse allowed the conquering empire to ensure any surviving humans were found and eradicated, without having to do the dirty work themselves. It was sick and depraved, but also brilliant. The hunted became the hunters. Human minds forced to kill humans.

Taylor's memories of his experiences while viewing the universe through the Hedalt's crooked lens were still vivid in his human mind, so much so that it was hard to believe none of it had been real. He remembered looking in the mirror and seeing the human face of his brain's original host staring back at him – the real Captain Taylor Ray. Now, he saw the silver simulant eyes of his true self. He had believed that Earth was still there, waiting for him to return home, wealthy and happy, after his four year deep-space recon mission, oblivious to the fact that the planet had been nuked over three hundred years earlier. But Taylor now knew the truth. He, unlike every other simulant in the galaxy, was awake – truly awake – and truly alive.

How it had happened was still a mystery; one that Taylor's new friend and snarky superior officer – and possibly sole-surviving human in the universe – Commander Sarah Sonner, was still investigating on their hijacked Corvette.

Sonner had been the only survivor of the Contingency – an ambitious and desperate plan set in motion by Earth Fleet to save the human race, once it was clear that the war against the Hedalt was unwinnable. The Contingency involved hiding a series of secret bases in the deepest and most unexplored regions of the galaxy. There, an elite group of officers and crew – the best Earth had left to offer – would remain in hibernation stasis while a vast automated shipyard built the Nimrod Fleet. Then when the time was right, Earth would strike back against the Hedalt in a co-ordinated surprise attack, throwing everything humanity had left at them in an effort to re-take Earth and blockade it against any further attempts at conquest. For fifty years they would wait, lying in stasis while the fleet was amassed; long enough, they believed, for the Hedalt to forget about human beings and lower their guard. But the Contingency had failed and three hundred and twenty-five years later Sonner was the only human to emerge from the failed stasis chambers.

By coincidence the malfunctioning equipment drew Taylor's curious Hunter simulant crew to investigate. Still under the influence of the Hedalt programming at the time, Taylor had been knocked unconscious while fighting what he believed to be a Hedalt solider, and woke again to see the world free of the veil imposed by the Hedalt's neurological engineering. He found that the Hedalt soldier was actually a human woman, Sarah Sonner. And he discovered – or rather, was forced by Sonner to confront – the true nature of what he was, too. But, it had all come too late for the rest of Taylor's crew; Blake, Casey and Satomi had been killed, before Taylor had learnt the truth, and before he had a chance to wake them. Taylor had agreed to help Sonner find the other Contingency bases, and re-light the fire of the plan to fight back against the Hedalt, but in truth he had little motivation to save a planet he'd never actually known. Earth belonged to the real Taylor, dead centuries earlier. His true purpose was to seek out and find other simulant recreations of his crew; find them, and wake them. Satomi Rose, most of all.

Satomi Rose... where are you now? Taylor wondered, attempting unsuccessfully to picture the face of his technical specialist. He glanced over his shoulder to the mission operations console, where Satomi would usually be found, diligently working away while also trying to block out the often incessant banter between Casey and Blake. *I wonder if you'll still know me? I wonder if you can accept what I am, and what you will become?*

Taylor had missed, botched or bottled so many opportunities to tell Satomi how he felt during their time together. Taylor had believed it to be four years, but the truth was he had no idea how long they'd all been out in space, hunting for signs of human existence. He knew now that their time together, and his interactions with the other members of his crew, had been fantasies played out by his engineered brain, but his feelings for Satomi remained, and still felt real. The difference now was that Taylor was alive, and if he could find Satomi – find her and free her – then perhaps they still had a chance. It was the longest of long shots, and he knew it, but it was all he had left. It was all he had to fight for. His crew were like his family.

In fact, Taylor's goal was arguably far more achievable than Sonner's ambition of finding living humans on the other two Contingency bases, and then defeating the Hedalt armada. That seemed like an impossible and frankly absurd proposition to Taylor, yet Sonner was undeterred, despite the strong possibility that she was the last human alive. In contrast, Taylor knew for certain that there was at least one other Satomi Rose in the galaxy, because he had spoken to her using his newfound, quasi-magical ability to enter the Fabric. But, whereas others needed starships to travel along the threads of this pan-galactic network, Taylor could navigate it using only his mind, giving him an ability to witness events half the galaxy away as if he were physically there. It was while he was inside the Fabric that he had spoken to Satomi. Again, like so much of what had happened to him in the last few days, Taylor had no idea how that had been possible, and also had no idea where this other Satomi was. But it had given him hope – hope enough to want to live on. And in the process of finding Satomi and the others, if he could strike back against the race that had twisted his mind and turned him into an assassin, so much the better.

Revenge was an ugly human emotion – Taylor knew that – but what the Hedalt had done was more repulsive still. Payback was due and he intended to claim it in full.

THREE

Taylor slipped around the side of the pilot's chair and sat down, re-checking the co-ordinates of their next jump; the third of five that they needed to make in order to reach the second Contingency base. The co-ordinates were locked in and the computations had been run and checked, but he decided to check them again, just to be sure. "I wish you were here, Casey," he said out loud, while entering the commands, "I'm still afraid I'm going to jump us inside a damn black hole..."

He finished the checks, still half-convinced he was going to jump them into oblivion, and rested back, sliding his hands into the creases of the seat. His synthetic fingers touched on something hard and square. He fumbled around and eventually managed to grab hold of the object and pluck it out. Taylor held it in front of his nose and laughed. "Contraband..." he grinned, staring at the mint, still neatly wrapped in its packaging. Then in a more theatrical timbre, he added, "Guilty as charged, miss Valera!" Taylor had always known that Casey would often sit on the bridge alone and suck on candies like this, flagrantly flouting the rule not to eat while on station, but he always let it slide, because it was Casey. It was just one of the many rules that his quirky pilot casually flouted without ever coming across as being insubordinate or disrespectful, such was her unique charm.

More surprising than actually discovering the mint tucked into the folds of the pilot's chair was the realization that it existed at all, considering Casey's simulant body could never have eaten them. This was one of the more mind-boggling aspects of the Hedalt's deception; the mix of pure fantasy with reality. Sonner had tried to explain this to him by stating that it was sometimes simply easier to recreate real objects rather than trick the brain into seeing something differently. It was the same reason that the bridge of his Hedalt Hunter Corvette had actually been made to look like that of an Earth Fleet Nimrod. But Sonner had also suggested that a physical connection to real objects may also have been important in maintaining the Hedalt fiction. *Perhaps mixing in a bit of truth with the lie helped to make the whole thing easier to swallow,* he wondered.

He held the mint between his thumb and forefinger, contemplating the absurdity of its existence like Rodin's *The Thinker*. But what was bugging him most of all was not knowing how many other candies Casey had lost or stashed away in other parts of the ship, like pirate treasure. Taylor liked to keep a clean house, and now everywhere he looked, he saw the potential for hidden candy wrappers and dusty old sweets.

It was then that the door slid open and Sonner breezed inside. "I think I understand more about how this Hedalt brain interface works," she blurted out, before spotting that Taylor appeared to be holding a wrapped-up candy to his face and studying it like a Greek philosopher. She stopped and scowled, "I didn't realize that simulants had a sweet tooth..."

Taylor pocketed the mint and spun the chair around to face Sonner. "Casey used to sit here and eat these, when the rest of us weren't around. She thought I never noticed, but of course I did." Laughing, he added, "I mean, she obviously didn't really eat them, she just pretended to eat them." Then he paused, realizing that this still wasn't right and corrected himself again, "I mean, she would have believed she ate them, but really she didn't... Hell, I can't keep this stuff straight!"

Sonner's scowl softened and the corner of her mouth turned up slightly. "Captain, you do realize that allowing crew to eat at their stations on the bridge is against regulations..."

Taylor shook his head, "Very funny. You ever heard of the phrase, 'don't sweat the small stuff?'"

"I have now," Sonner replied, continuing onto the bridge and resting with her back against the pilot's console. "Personally, I've always found that it's the smallest details that are often the most consequential."

"That's not what the phrase means..."

"I know what it means, Captain," said Sonner, gently slapping Taylor on the shoulder with the back of her hand, "but, as it happens, that elicit candy actually ties in to why I wanted to speak with you."

"Oh, really?" said Taylor, sitting more upright in the chair; it was a random but intriguing coincidence, "How so?"

"I still have more detailed analyses to perform," Sonner began, careful to not sound too definitive, "but I think my original theory was on the money. They appear to act like physical anchors to your host's human past. They help stop the brain from rejecting what would otherwise be a sham reality."

Taylor stroked his chin; a reflex action carried over from a time when he actually believed he had stubble there, "I was actually just thinking the same thing, before you walked in."

Sonner scowled. "Hey, don't try to steal my thunder, Captain."

"You're not the only smart ass on this ship, you know..."

Sonner smiled. "Do you want to show me your detailed scientific analysis, or shall I go first?"

"I'll allow you to go first..." Taylor answered, playing along.

Sonner's eyes narrowed and she nodded, "Uh huh, thought so..." She swiveled around to face the console, entering a short sequence of commands. A second later a detailed anatomical illustration of a brain appeared on the viewport. Taylor recoiled slightly, grateful that his simulant stomach didn't churn in the same way a human gut would. Sonner saw his reaction, and laughed. "I didn't peg you for squeamish."

"I prefer not to see the insides of people, if at all possible," Taylor replied, annoyed that his reaction seemed to amuse Sonner.

"Well, if you can hold onto your lunch for long enough, you might learn something," Sonner went on, unsympathetically. Then she pressed a button on the console and the brain lit up with swirling blue patterns of varying shades. "This is your brain activity when in stasis; what I'd call your 'sleep mode'. I pulled the data records from the computer system."

"Is that really my brain?" Taylor asked, still scowling, but Sonner just shushed him and continued.

"As you can see the activity level is fairly low, and also not every part of your brain is active," Sonner went on, before pressing another button on the console, which switched the image to one with patterns of blue and green. "This is your brain activity when in simulant mode; as in when your cranial unit..."

"My cranial unit?" Taylor interrupted, offended at how Sonner so easily talked about him like an object she had bought from a hardware store.

"Fine, Captain Touchy," Sonner carried on, irritated at the interruption, "this is when your 'head' was attached to your simulant body and you were physically interacting with the ship and crew, prior to a ground mission." Then she added, almost as an afterthought, "This is before you broke free of the Hedalt's hold on your mind, of course."

Taylor looked at the new patterns, which occupied almost all of the brain, and seemed to have a higher frequency of darker-colored areas. "So, you're saying my brain was more active while I was roaming around in this body?"

"You catch on quick, Captain!" said Sonner, with mock admiration. "It seems that interacting with familiar objects is the equivalent of exercising your brain and keeping it healthy."

Taylor nodded, "Living in the dream state is not enough. We need something tangible too."

"Right again," said Sonner, smiling, and actually not sounding condescending for a change. "Now, look at this..." Sonner hit another button and the image switched again. This time the brain was lit up mostly in red with patches of blue and green, and the swirling motion of the patterns had intensified, as if he was now looking at a radar picture of a tropical storm raging inside his head.

"What's going on there?" asked Taylor, recoiling slightly again at the thought of his brain fizzing like an unstable fusion reactor.

"That was your brain activity during the time you were jaunting through the Fabric, a day or so ago," said Sonner, whose excitement level had increased with each new image.

"Is it supposed to look quite so..." Taylor struggled for an accurate word to describe what he was seeing, "angry?"

"I have no idea what it's supposed to look like, Captain, but if this were the brain activity of a normal human, I'd say we were looking at an amalgamation of Einstein, Monet, da Vinci and Hawking all at once."

Taylor grinned, "So, you're saying I'm a bonafide genius?"

"I wouldn't go that far," said Sonner, studying

the image for a few more seconds, before switching the viewport off, "but you're certainly not normal, that's for damn certain."

"Tell me something I don't already know…"

"Okay, try this," said Sonner with a sparkle in her voice that he'd not heard before. "I think finding a highly personal item from each of your crew could help with waking them up, in the same way you are now."

Taylor leaned forward; now he really was interested. "In what way?"

"Have you ever heard about how people in comas can be helped back to consciousness sooner by hearing familiar voices?" said Sonner.

"Can't say that I have," Taylor shrugged.

"Well, they can," Sonner went on, undeterred by Taylor's ignorance. "The voices stimulate long-term memories and trigger awareness. I think these objects can do the same and be a catalyst that helps bring the simulant brain out of its induced state, and allow it to adjust to the new reality. If I can engineer a suitable environment to nurture the shift."

"But, that doesn't explain me," said Taylor, not following Sonner's argument. "I fell off a stack of containers in the hangar on the Contingency base, and when I came around, everything was different. There was no catalyst for me."

"Yes, there was, in a way at least," said Sonner,

"It was all around you. The voices of your crew. The sight of an Earth Fleet hangar and rows of Nimrods; all of that was familiar to your brain. The brain of the original Taylor Ray, I mean, which yours is a faithful reproduction of."

"But what actually caused me to wake up?"

"I'm not entirely sure yet," admitted Sonner, "But clearly the impact shook something loose. I'm still running before-and-after comparisons on the scans of your cranial unit, after which I hope to know more."

"Can you please stop using the words 'cranial unit'?" said Taylor wincing.

"Sorry, I meant your head."

"I know what you meant," said Taylor, crossly, "but can you try to refrain from talking about me as if I'm just another tool in the workshop?"

"My, my, we really are touchy today, aren't we Captain?" teased Sonner, pushing off from the console and heading back into the center of the bridge. "Hold onto that candy, Captain," she said, pointing towards Taylor's pocket. "You might need it, if we ever bump into another Casey. And, I'd advise finding personal items for each of the others too. If we ever get a chance to grab one, and I figure out how to break the Hedalt spell over them, we'll need something familiar to help trigger that spark of awareness. Understand?"

"Commander, I honestly have no idea what

you're talking about," said Taylor, still smarting from Sonner's lack of sympathy and tact regarding his 'cranial unit', "but I trust that you do, so that will have to do, I suppose."

"Stop it, you're making me blush," said Sonner, sarcastically, dropping into the command chair. "Are we ready to make the next jump?"

"Yes, I'm primed and ready to squash our atoms into oblivion again at your command."

"Very well, start the jump sequence, Captain," said Sonner, gripping the arms of the chair. Taylor had observed that Sonner enjoyed super-luminal travel even less than he did, and probably even less than the average Hedalt did. Considering that a long super-luminal jump could actually kill an average Hedalt, that was saying something. "We only have this and one more long hop along a thread of the Fabric, before we're within blind-jump range of the second Contingency base."

Taylor rigged the ship for super-luminal travel and spooled up the jump engines, which would propel them thousands of light-years to another super-luminal transceiver. Jumping along the threads allowed ships to travel far further than was safely possible using a blind jump, where the end point had to be calculated with significantly greater precision. Long blind jumps also ran the risk of ending up in the wrong part of the galaxy, or worse, inside a nebula or star, or some other galactic body that was inhospitable to space ships.

"Squash our atoms when ready..." said Sonner, through gritted teeth.

"Aye aye, Commander Sarah Sonner," replied Taylor, and then he initiated the countdown.

"Jumping in five..."

...F o u r

...T h r e e

... T w o

. . . O n e

Taylor shut his silver eyes as the spinning sensation began, whirling his mind like a tornado. And then he felt the bridge collapse in on itself, squashing it, himself and Sonner out of existence, save for their disembodied consciousnesses. He could feel Sonner's presence, but unlike previous jumps, he could feel another presence too; distant, but familiar. It was similar, he realized, to how he felt while inside the translucent deep space corridor, beyond the starlight door. In that place his mind could reach out into the Fabric; into the in-between space where he now briefly existed as the ship jumped along a thread to another super-luminal transceiver.

Satomi? he thought, *is that you? Are you there?* But there was no time for a response as the bridge burst into existence again, and he was back in the pilot's chair, hearing and feeling the deep thrum of the jump engines winding down.

He opened his eyes, looked up at the main viewport, and froze. "Commander..." There was no answer. Taylor looked behind him to see Sonner holding her temples, looking dazed and more than a little queasy, as if someone had just spun her around and around in her chair. "Sarah..." he said, and the more familiar tone got her attention.

"Sarah?" she repeated, opening her eyes and peering down her nose at him. "Only my ex-husband ever called me Sarah."

"What the hell did everyone else call you then?" asked Taylor, before realizing he didn't actually care to know the answer, "Never mind, just look at the viewport," he said, pointing up at the giant screen.

Sonner looked and then sprang out of her chair. Hanging in space, like a medieval morning star, was the super-luminal transceiver they had expected to find, but next to it, a hundred times larger, was a sprawling space station. Though calling it a space station was like calling a lake a paddling pool; it was more like a city in space.

"Is that a Hedalt space station?" asked Taylor, though he was not hopeful of getting the answer he wanted.

Sonner puckered her lips and then placed her hands on her hips, "Damned if I know, Captain, but if it is then we have a problem..."

FOUR

The jump engines spun down, emanating a slowly descending whine that hummed though the cold, metal deck plating of Provost Adra's powerful frigate. But Adjutant Lux did not hear the sound; he was gripping the framework of the pilot's chairs to either side of his station, bent double, face contorted in agony, as if someone had been repeatedly kicking him in the gut.

Adra herself had also been unable to remain standing, and had dropped to one knee, one hand pressed against the deck plating, her fingernails raking against the diamond-studded surface. The pain and disorientation caused by the super-luminal jump had hit her like a tidal wave, stealing her breath and strength. She remained on one knee, tensing all her muscles in an effort to regain

34

control of her body, all the time keeping a watchful eye on Lux, anxious to ensure he did not see her weakened. *Stand! Stand up!* she called out in her mind, and then with all the force of her will she pushed herself upright, straight as an arrow, body still flooded with pain, and waited for Lux to recover. It was not vanity that made Adra want to recuperate first and prevent her junior from seeing her in discomfort; a provost was expected to be stronger, and to show strength at all times. It was also a matter of personal pride and honor.

Several more seconds passed before Lux finally managed to stand unaided. He straightened the armored jacket that formed part of his obsidian-black uniform as best he could considering that his hands and arms burned like acid and quivered like a frightened animal. Then he turned to face Adra, pushing his hands down by his sides, fists clenched tightly together. "Jump complete, Provost," he said, his voice betraying the strain his body still endured, "I am analyzing our position now."

Adra nodded, but didn't respond with words, conscious that her own voice may also betray signs of stress. Fortunately Lux didn't wait for a reply, instead turning back to study the consoles at either side of the simulant pilots, which now sat dead still, waiting for further instructions.

With Lux's back turned, Adra allowed her posture to sag a little. She may have been one of only a tiny fraction of the Hedalt population that possessed the rare genetic mutation and the physical strength to endure the rigors of space travel – one of the reasons she had been assigned command of a War Frigate in the first instance – but it was a grueling and debilitating experience nonetheless. She cursed the race of augmented beings that had engineered this weakness into the Hedalt genetic code millennia ago, as a way of imprisoning them on the planets and Way Stations they had been bound to as slaves. Although her ancestors had risen up against and overthrown their masters and captors long ago, this genetic shackle remained a part of every Hedalt's DNA, despite determined attempts to cure it.

Adra took a succession of slow, deep breaths, feeling her vitality returning, and then peered up at the halo of screens that surrounded her command platform. Displayed on one of the screens was the signal anomaly they had encountered before being ordered away on a Priority One matter to escort the high-value freighters. The longer she studied the patterns, the more Adra was convinced that they represented brainwave patterns from a high-functioning simulant; a human mind that had somehow managed to break free of its programming and infiltrate the Fabric. How or why were questions that burned in Adra's mind, but these questions were secondary to the need to find the simulant and destroy it. The prospect of a human consciousness roaming freely inside the CoreNet – the system that stitched the Hedalt Empire together – was too great to ignore, as was the even more troubling prospect that it may not have been operating alone. Warfare Command may have been convinced that the human race had been exterminated long ago, but Adra considered this thinking to be dangerous complacency and hubris. Humans were a virus, and like many viruses, they had a way of surviving.

Adra was also acutely aware that her peers at Warfare Command would view her theories with deep skepticism. Convinced that the human race had been made extinct centuries ago, Warfare Command had already decommissioned almost all the Hunter Corvettes, which were crewed by the high-functioning simulants that Adra herself developed. And if it was the case that one of these simulant crew members had become aware of its true nature, and now posed a threat to the CoreNet, and the Empire as a whole, Adra would be blamed. This was the reason why she had withheld the information from her peers and from the High Provost himself, and instead instructed Adjutant Lux to attempt to locate the source of the anomaly. She would get to the bottom of this mystery herself, and deal with it personally.

Frustratingly for Adra, the closest point they could trace the signal anomaly back to was a distant super-luminal transceiver located in the inner section of the Scutum-Crux arm, close to the intersection with the galactic long bar. This transceiver encompassed a vast region of space, so in itself was not helpful in pinpointing the origin with even the slightest degree of accuracy. Adra had made Lux re-check the calculations to be certain of the location, partly because she was still not yet fully confident in her new Adjutant's abilities, but also because it was a desolate and unexplored region of the galaxy. The super-luminal transceiver was on the very fringe of the Fabric. To move beyond it, closer towards the galactic center, would mean increasingly riskier, not to mention more painful, blind jumps.

Adra swiped her hand to the right, causing the halo of screens above her to rotate by thirty degrees, bringing a new set of information into the Provost's field of view. She studied the data in silence as the simulants on the bridge milled from station to station, wordlessly conducting all the core tasks of starship operation, which Adra and Lux could not have done on their own. As a result, they were the only two Hedalt officers on the entire ship, which could easily have sustained a crew of three hundred. Adra swiped her hand right again, bringing a new group of screens and a new set of information into view. Adra's quick mind and scientific expertise allowed her to analyze the vast swathes of data quickly, and one of the updated readings immediately caught her attention. She reached up towards the screen and pulled her hand back towards her sternum, causing the screen to descend on a spindly metal arm and hang in front of her like a heavy fruit on a long, willowy branch.

"The updated scans have detected another faint transmission emanating from a system nearby," said Adra, addressing Lux, but keeping her eyes on the screen.

Lux moved beside the command platform, swiftly enough so that Adra would not consider him to be dallying, but measuring his pace carefully enough that she also didn't consider him over-eager or rash. Lux was acutely aware that he had yet to impress Adra, and if he was ever to rise through the ranks to Vice Provost and perhaps one day even to Provost himself, a recommendation from a former commander was essential. Lux stood dutifully and examined the information on the screen dangling in front of Adra.

"It is the CoreNet transmission from a ship's transceiver," said Lux, betraying his obvious surprise at the result of his own analysis. He had assumed that Adra was referring to another signal anomaly, such as the one caused by the simulant brainwaves.

"Well observed, Adjutant Lux," said Adra, though if it was intended as praise, it did not come across as such to Lux's ears. "Compile the current positions of any remaining Hunter Corvettes and send their locations to me."

"Yes, Provost," Lux answered without delay, but then added, feeling a little emboldened by his correct analysis of the data, "Is it still your belief that the anomaly is caused by some sort of rogue or malfunctioning simulant?"

"I don't deal in belief, Adjutant, and neither should you," said Adra, dismissively. "Facts are what matter. Now, get me that data."

"Yes, Provost," said Lux, a little crestfallen, but hiding it well. He paced reticently back to his station, aware that he had yet again failed to make a good impression on his commander. And he was even more acutely aware that there was a good chance Adra would force him to endure a third agonizing jump in as many hours.

Adra was about to wave the screen away when the data updated again, showing a more detailed analysis of the transceiver transmission, and also the star system from where it had originated. She recognized the transmission instantly, because she had designed it. It was unique to the transceivers installed in Hunter Corvettes. The star system itself, however, was unknown to Adra. It was a wholly unremarkable system with an ancient, red giant star and six barren, lifeless planets. But she also knew that if the transceiver was from a Hunter Corvette, it suggested the ship had detected a possible human base or colony. She knew that she was reaching and making assumptions, but when it came to human beings, she took no chances. She sent the co-ordinates to Lux's console and then waved the screen away, before calling out, "Calculate a jump to these co-ordinates, Adjutant Lux."

Lux saw the data appear on his console and processed the blind jump needed to reach the star system. He relayed the information to the primary pilot simulant, before turning to face Adra. "Course locked in, Provost Adra."

Adra could already hear the whine of the jump engines building all around her. She clenched her fists tightly together, steeling herself for the pain that would soon follow, and took a long, deep breath in, before slowly letting it escape her lips like the rasp of wind wheezing through a cracked window pane.

"Jump."

FIVE

The mission operations console bleeped an alert and Taylor instinctively swiveled his pilot's chair towards it, ready to ask Satomi what was up, but of course she wasn't there, and the sudden reminder of this stung. He continued to swivel so that he was facing Sonner instead, attempting to make it look as though this had been his intention all along. Thankfully, Sonner had also noticed the alert and was already on her way over to the mission ops station, which spared him any embarrassment.

"We're receiving a message," said Sonner, the surprise evident in her voice.

Taylor got up and joined her, his simulant brow furrowing, "A message from whom?"

"From that hulk of a space city out there,"

Sonner answered, thought it sounded like she hardly believed it herself. "They are inviting us to dock, and have relayed landing instructions."

Taylor huffed a laugh, "Well, I guess from their point of view, we're just another Hedalt ship. I keep forgetting, because of this damned fake Nimrod bridge."

"It's a good job we are a sheep in wolf's clothing," Sonner answered, twisting the adage on its head, "otherwise, we'd probably already have a dozen cannons aimed right at us."

"Are you sure that's a Hedalt space station?" said Taylor, still struggling to process the scale of the object on the viewport. "I thought you told me the Hedalt couldn't hack space travel, hence the likes of me?"

"I don't know who else is over there if not the Hedalt," Sonner replied. "During the war we never saw evidence of little green men or anyone else. It was just us and those evil bastards."

"Maybe they just got over their dislike of space?"

"I doubt it, from what we know it was more ingrained than that," Sonner replied. Now that she'd suggested the possibility, she was keeping a careful watch on the station to make there weren't any cannons swinging in their direction. "But, remember that there are probably tens of billions of Hedalt in the galaxy now; even if only a thousandth of a percent could hack space travel, we're still looking at numbers in the hundreds of thousands, or more."

Taylor chewed this over and realized it made sense. In some ways it was good to know that a relative minority of Hedalt were out in the galaxy, because it was fewer of them to fight, but if Sonner was right then even a thousandth of a percent still outnumbered them by many orders of magnitude, even assuming they could find and rescue people from the other Contingency bases.

"Well, I don't know about you, but I don't really fancy a family reunion with my illustrious creators right now," said Taylor, "So, how about we just high-tail it out of here instead?"

"Suits me just fine, Captain," said Sonner, dropping into the mission ops chair and starting to type the response, while Taylor began to make preparations to jump away. He glanced back to check on Sonner and for a brief moment, he saw Satomi instead. Though Sonner wore her hair differently, it was a similar color to Satomi's and the Earth Fleet uniform plus their similar physiques was enough to trick Taylor's human brain. If he'd still had a heart, he was sure it would have leapt into his throat.

Sonner noticed Taylor peering over, plus the startled look on his simulant face, "Something the matter Captain? Usually, when I catch guys staring at me, they don't like what comes next."

Taylor sat back in the chair and smiled, "You just reminded me of someone, that's all. Besides, there's nothing down here for you to bust, anymore," he added, indicating to his lap.

Sonner frowned, "Seriously, Captain, that's way too much information."

"Can you just send the damn message so we can get out of here?" Taylor laughed, while swinging his chair back and peering up at the giant space city again. Though now that he looked more closely, it didn't look in particularly good condition. There were numerous sections that showed obvious signs of damage and decay, some of which had been crudely patched up and others left unrepaired, while there were still other sections that appeared to be in such a bad state that they had been completely shut down. Overall, the configuration reminded him of the old naval aircraft carriers that used to command the seas on Earth in the early twenty-first century, except that it was about a hundred times the size. There was a large top deck, where ships could be seen landing before being swallowed into the city's underbelly. Structures towered above it, though there seemed to be no plan or order as to how and where these were constructed. It was as if multiple different architects and engineers had designed and built them on over a span of decades or even longer.

The station also appeared to extend deep into the hulk beneath the deck, which is where most of the damage seemed to be concentrated, with the upper levels looking in much better condition.

"This place looks pretty beat up," Taylor commented out loud.

"What were you expecting; some sort of pristine utopia?" said Sonner, testily.

Taylor was sure that Sonner's condescension was never meant nastily, and was simply a facet of her spiky persona, but it still got under his simulated skin. "Well, yes, actually, I was. They are the conquerors, after all, with an empire spanning the galaxy."

Sonner glanced up at the image of the space city on the viewport. Her knowledge was centuries out of date, but even towards the end of the war, over three hundred years ago, Earth Fleet had known there were distinct classes in Hedalt civilization. The military ruling class was at the top of the pile, but she had to admit that the condition of the city did look rough considering the Hedalt's vast resources, especially after taking Earth. She initiated a scan of the station to get some more information, but kept the energy level low so as to not attract too much attention.

"I'm a woman out of time here," Sonner eventually answered, "but there were strong indications of deep social stratification in Hedalt civilization. Sadly, I didn't learn much before they put me on ice."

Taylor thought about asking when Sonner's frosty personality was finally going to thaw out, but thought better of it.

"Besides, we're out at the ass-end of nowhere here; I doubt this is the most desirable property location in the Hedalt empire."

Taylor grunted an acknowledgment and continued to make calculations for the next jump, but then he noticed something unusual; he couldn't establish a navigational link to the super-luminal transceiver that hung in front of them like a giant wrecking ball. He tried again, but the link was rejected.

"Hey, we have a problem," Taylor called back to Sonner, "I can't sync our navigation system with the transceiver out there, and without a nav link, we can't jump. At least not along the threads."

"Damn it," he heard Sonner utter and she slammed her palm on the console.

Taylor spun the chair around, surprised by the strength of Sonner's reaction, considering so far she had dealt with adversity with amazing coolness. "It's not that big a deal; we can cover the distance in blind jumps instead. It'll take longer, but should be okay."

"Not in this ship, Captain," said Sonner, bleakly. "This Corvette's blind jump range is limited; it would take maybe ten hops just to reach just the next super-luminal transceiver along our flight plan. And it's an old ship, remember; if we blew the jump drive out in deep space, we'd be truly screwed."

Taylor suddenly understood the gravity of their predicament. He got up and joined Sonner again at the mission ops console, searching the corners of his mind for possible solutions. Now, more than ever, he wished Satomi was there; this was exactly the sort of tangled knot that she was expert at unpicking. "We could push the red line; it's riskier, but it might be enough to cut that to four or five jumps. Then we give it time to cool off, before jumping again."

Sonner cocked her head and half-shrugged, half-winced, "Maybe, but it's still a hell of a risk. I can fix a lot of stuff out in space, especially with my new mechanical friends from the Contingency base, but jump drives are finicky creatures, and this ship's drive and I aren't best friends yet."

Taylor had forgotten that despite the bridge layout mimicking that of an Earth Fleet Nimrod-class cruiser, their ship was actually a Hedalt design and not something that Sonner had any expertise with. Then he glanced down at the console Sonner was working on and saw the scan data. "You probed the station?" he said, with admiration; it was a gutsy move that could be construed as aggressive or suspicious, if they'd been detected. "Did you find out anything useful?"

"Interesting, yes. Useful? I don't know yet."

"What do you have?"

Sonner slid her chair over to the comms section and brought up the brief exchange of messages that had been transmitted between her and the space city so far. "When they transmitted their docking instructions, I declined the invitation and explained that we'd be jumping on. Look at the reply."

Taylor instinctively leaned in closer to the screen to read the small lines of text, but as he did so he realized he could already read it from where he was standing; his simulant eyes may have looked like balls of mercury, but they were keener than a hawk's. The message from the station read, 'Acknowledged, Contingency One. Approach jump line and transmit validation key when ready.' Taylor massaged the silken smooth polymer that covered his chin, in place of the usual stubble. "Why did they call us Contingency One?"

"We put our transceiver onto the Nimrod we crashed into the planet, remember?" Sonner replied, "So I had to make up a name on the spot."

"Don't you think that calling the ship 'Contingency One' is a bit like painting a bright red target on hull?"

"Relax, Captain, I doubt the Hedalt even have a

word for 'contingency'," said Sonner, dismissively. "Anyway, you're focusing on the wrong part of the damn message."

Taylor read the message again and spotted the section Sonner was referring to, "Transmit validation? What does that mean?"

"It means we're up the proverbial creek, Captain," said Sonner, dolefully. "This must be some kind of toll booth or checkpoint; to get through we need to have the proper identification, otherwise they won't let us tap our nav into the super-luminal transceiver."

Taylor suddenly realized the problem, "Right, and our validation key went boom along with the Nimrod we crashed."

"Bingo, Captain," said Sonner, brightly, "and without a proper validation key, we can't jump along the threads from this marker."

"So, we build another transceiver," said Taylor, making it sound like an obvious solution. "You're the engineering wizard; no problem, right?"

"You Earth Fleet Captains are all the same," said Sonner, shaking her head, "You sit in the big chairs and consider these ships your own, but haven't the faintest idea how they're bolted together. I'm afraid, it's not that easy, fly boy."

"Okay, so what's your plan, genius?" Taylor replied, flexing some spines of his own.

Sonner sniffed and then fixed Taylor with a

laser-like stare. "We will have to dock on that hulking city out there and steal us a transceiver."

"What?!"

"It's the only way, unless you want to hop around the galactic long belt for the next few weeks, until this Hedalt piece of crap inevitably breaks down."

Taylor folder his arms and shook his head in disbelief. "You're crazy."

"And you're a robot who thinks he's human. We make a fine pair. So, what do you say?"

"How do you know there's even a transceiver on the station that we could steal?" said Taylor, avoiding the question.

"I scanned it, remember?" Sonner answered, tapping her temple with her index finger, "Besides, that thing is over three kilometers across; there has to be somewhere or someone on that hulk that has what we need."

Taylor shook his head again, and considered their options, before swiftly coming to the conclusion that they had none. He glowered down at Sonner, "I'm going to regret ever meeting you."

SIX

The War Frigate lurched out of the Fabric and was immediately bathed in the soft ruby glow of a red giant. But Adra did not see the new star; she was blinded by the fierce pounding inside her head that felt like a jackhammer drilling into her skull.

Adra staggered forward, but she fought to keep her balance and remained standing. The pain and nausea resulting from three jumps in such close proximity was nearly overwhelming, and she clenched her jaw so tightly in an effort to ward it off that her teeth creaked under the strain. At the front of the bridge, Lux had buckled to his knees, still clutching the bare metal frames of the pilot's chairs, which were all that prevented him from toppling completely. Adra relaxed her aching jaw and forced her breathing into rhythmic inhalations and exhalations and eventually the discomfort began to ease.

"Report, Adjutant Lux," Adra called out, using all her strength to compose the words clearly and without any hint of strain, knowing that Lux was in no condition to reply. She wanted to keep her new adjutant on his toes; to force him to react quicker and to learn to deal with the pain without it affecting his performance. She watched as he clawed himself upright, the effort almost as excruciating to watch as it must have felt. When he spoke, it was like the words had been raked from his throat through torture.

"Jump... complete," Lux began, only half-turning to face Adra – he did not want her to see his contorted expression. He then paused to take several rapid breaths and continued. "We are holding at approximately seventeen million kilometers from the sixth planet." The Adjutant released his vice-like hold on the chairs and forced his back to straighten, before twisting to face his commander fully. He would rather have stayed looking away, but to address a provost without facing them was a mark of disrespect. "The signal is emanating from the fourth planet."

"Take us there," said Adra, briefly glancing up at the flood of new information appearing on the screens above her. Lux nodded and relayed the order to the primary pilot simulant, which immediately carried out the command, before he again steadied himself on the back of its chair.

The thrum of the engines powering up replaced the near silence on the bridge, and Adra found the sudden influx of sound and the accompanying mechanical beat through the deck plating to be soothing and an aid to concentration. She hated the sterile atmosphere on the frigate and the near-constant white noise that seemed to bore into her skull, making her long more than ever to be back on a planet. The command of a War Frigate was not her first choice of duty, or even her second, despite the prestige that came with it, in addition to the coveted rank of provost. The rank was the only reason she had accepted the post, because while it was possible to attain the position of full provost in a non-operational role, such as in the scientific sub-service that Adra belonged to, the chances were so rare as to be essentially non-existent. But as a provost, Adra was granted a position amongst the Hedalt elite inner circle, and the opportunity in the future to explore her passion, which was the study of the true ancestry of her race. Importantly, this was a passion that she could pursue with both feet firmly planted on soil, rather than metal deck plates.

To Adra, nothing was more important than the study of Hedalt history. It was a history that had forever been altered from its natural destiny hundreds of thousands of years earlier by the alien species that had taken their ancestors from their home world and forced them into bondage. Yet, despite the passing of eons since that event, the Hedalt had never known the name of the species that had enslaved them, calling them simply the Masters.

Now all that remained of the Masters were the simulant frames that had once housed the brains of these hyper-advanced beings. Through an ability to blend technology with biology, the Masters had achieved near-immortality inside bodies that neither aged nor decayed. Instead of procreation the Masters chose replication, growing new copies of their brains when the existing ones degenerated beyond healing. But, as the eons elapsed and the countless iterations of artificial replication lead to irreparable brain damage, the Masters gradually relied on sophisticated neural implants to keep themselves alive. For tens of thousands of years the Hedalt had served as the Masters' indentured workers, with no prospect or hope of being set free. But, eventually, the Masters' deteriorating organic components could no longer be salvaged by technology, leading to widespread failures and fatalities that whittled away their numbers until the Hedalt were able to rise against them. After a hard-fought war the Hedalt managed to capture an ancient installation called the Nexus and take control of the Masters' central network – the CoreNet – which was the foundation of their blended technological and biological existence. Without the CoreNet the Masters were unable to function; those on planets were quickly and violently wiped out, while for the others scattered around the galaxy on ships or Way Stations, the loss of the CoreNet was akin to severing all nerve connections to the brain, killing them but leaving their simulant frames intact.

Once the Masters had been wiped out, the Hedalt reestablished the CoreNet, and set to work on the task of pressing the simulant frames into their service instead. Unfortunately, the simulant technology was so far beyond the Hedalt's understanding that reactivating the frames proved to be a difficult and laborious process. And without the core organic component – a brain – their usefulness was also limited.

But if the Hedalt were ever to take over the full extent of the Masters' territory, engineering fully-functioning simulants was a necessity. Careful to ensure their servants could not escape, the Masters had genetically-modified Hedalt brains to make them incompatible with both simulant technology and the interconnecting Fabric that joined them – the sub-layer of space through which the CoreNet operated. The most significant side-effect was that super-luminal travel was fatal to most Hedalt, making it impossible to fully man the ships required to expand their new empire. A tiny minority of Hedalt possessed a freak mutation that enabled them to endure jumps, and the strongest of these quickly rose to power, claiming outposts and Way Stations for their own, plus the resources they contained. This band of ruthless, elite Hedalt soldiers then banded together to form Warfare Command, and assumed supreme authority over the entire Hedalt race.

It was Warfare Command that began the experiments to create a new type of simulant. The initial trials used modified Hedalt brains in an effort to circumvent the Masters' safeguards, but these efforts proved fruitless. For hundreds of years the Hedalt tried and failed, even attempting genetic experiments with the brains of convicted Hedalt criminals. But the grotesque failure of these experiments was only matched by the nightmarish consequences for the unlucky souls whose brains were forced to endure inside the simulant bodies, if only for a short time before their agonizing and tormented demise. The experiments with Hedalt brains were also met with anger and unrest by the newly flourishing Hedalt society, which saw simulants as a symbol of the millennia of suffering they had been forced to endure.

However, as hope of using simulants as a means

through which the Hedalt could conquer the stars faded, Earth was discovered, and with it the mystery surrounding the origin of the Hedalt species was revealed. Earth was the true ancestral home of the Hedalt race; the planet that the Masters had used for their own dark purposes, long before homo sapiens had existed. A new opportunity presented itself; a chance to not only take back their rightful homeworld, but harvest the vital resource needed to create legions of simulant workers – human brains.

Many had argued against the proposal, saying that harvesting human brains to use as the core component of simulants would make the Hedalt no different to the Masters that had enslaved them, but these voices were quelled by the far stronger voices from the ruling Warfare Command. Adra's voice had been amongst them, and it was her research that allowed human biology to be successfully adapted for use in simulants. She felt no moral ambiguity over the decision. To Adra, it was simply nature restoring the true order of things, placing the Hedalt back into their rightful position as masters of Earth – a position that had been stolen from them by the race that had enslaved her ancestors.

After initially posing as benevolent interstellar neighbors in order to amass their forces over a period of years, The Hedalt assault of Earth took the humans completely by surprise. Even with their limited numbers, the devastating losses inflicted on Earth Fleet during the first hours of the war were enough to seal Earth's fate.

As the brilliant scientist who had adapted simulant technology to human biology, Adra was also acutely aware of the capabilities of the simulant frames, and the danger of their control mechanisms failing. Most had forgotten how powerful the Masters had been, both physically and in their cognitive abilities. But Adra had not forgotten and her apprehension over a human mind seizing full control over this ancient technology, even to the point of potentially being able to manipulate the CoreNet, was sufficient motivation for her to disobey orders and risk her coveted rank by going in search of the anomaly.

"Approaching the fourth planet in the system, Provost," said a visibly more composed Lux, turning to address her. Adra was moderately impressed at his speed of recovery, which at least showed signs of promise for the eager young Adjutant. "The signal appears to be coming from the surface."

"Take us into a low orbit directly above the location," Adra responded, but then she noticed that the ship was already on course; Lux apparently having anticipated her order. This annoyed her slightly, since the command had not been given, but she forgave his over-eagerness on this occasion, since it meant she would have her answers sooner. Lux bustled between his and several other simulant-crewed bridge stations, directing the analysis, and Adra saw the initial results appear on the screens above her. Then the reversing engines fired, changing the tone and rhythm of the beat through the deck plating as the bleak, brown planet engulfed the main viewport.

Adra stepped off the command platform and stood beside Lux at one of the science stations. Lux seemed about to speak, but then an alert sounded from the communications station and he left to deal with it. Adra observed Lux in her peripheral vision, but concentrated on the information appearing on the science console. *Crash debris...* she concluded, and her rapid assimilation of the remaining data confirmed her suspicions; the transceiver signal was definitely from an old Corvette-class cruiser – a Hunter.

Lux returned, but remained a respectful distance away and waited for Adra to invite him to speak, which she eventually did. "Only three Hunter Corvettes remain," Lux began, but before he could continue, Adra cut across him.

"Three?" she repeated, incredulously, "Three in the entire galaxy?"

"Yes, Provost," Lux confirmed. He was puzzled by Adra's reaction, but careful not to show it.

"Warfare Command reports that they recently lost contact with one of these three. It was assumed destroyed, due to age and decay."

Adra shook her head and clenched her teeth. *Age and decay...* she thought. *The High Provost's arrogance allowed our Hunters to wither, while the threat never truly died...*

"The last reported location confirms that the vessel had recently arrived at the super-luminal transceiver close to this system," Lux continued, oblivious to Adra's silent fury. "I calculate that this system is just within the blind jump range of a Corvette-class cruiser."

Adra leant forward, shoving the simulant crew member aside, and entered a sequence of commands into the science console before stepping back and peering up at the main viewport. A heavily-magnified image of the crash site appeared on the screen. Lux turned to stare up at it, but was careful to not comment, surmising from his previous attempts to engage with his commander that Adra would not welcome his unsolicited input.

"The signal anomaly," Adra continued, staring at the sprawling mass of ship debris through narrowed eyes, "was it detected before or after contact was lost with this ship?"

"It is difficult to be certain, but relative to the central CoreNet reference frame, I believe contact was lost with the Hunter Corvette before the signal anomaly was detected," said Lux. "The ship's transceiver link was then reestablished sometime after."

Adra returned her attention to the science console and scrutinized the information again. The transceiver signal was definitely that of a Hunter Corvette, of that there was no question, and the mass of debris suggested a vessel of a size consistent with a Corvette-class cruiser, but she could still not be completely certain that the debris was that of a Corvette. *But what else could it be?* Adra challenged herself, unsure as to why she would even question the data, given that all evidence pointed to it being their missing ship.

Nevertheless, the proximity of the anomaly to this missing ship continued to vex her. Given the vast scale of the galaxy, the chances of the mysterious signal anomaly appearing in the same outlying region of the Fabric as a ship crewed exclusively by high-functioning simulants seemed too remote to be purely coincidental. Adra knew from her own work and experience that simulant technology was built on the same foundations as the CoreNet, and therefore had the potential to access it. That Adra had disabled key neural components from the simulant cranial units meant that it should not have been possible for a simulant to influence the CoreNet. There had never been an incidence or even suggestion of this happening before. Yet Adra could not shake the feeling that the signal anomaly and the disappearance of the Hunter Corvette were directly related.

Several minutes passed in silence, during which time Lux attended the other stations on the bridge, quietly keeping himself busy while his commander was deep in thought. The diligent performance of his duties was only interrupted by an incoming message alert from Warfare Command. Lux abandoned his current task and moved swiftly to the communications console to read the message. 'War Frigate Adra, presence required at escort rendezvous as ordered. Explain absence and report arrival time immediately.' Lux scowled at the message; as the Adjutant, he was not privy to the orders from Warfare Command, unless the Provost deemed it necessary to pass them on. In this case, Provost Adra clearly had not thought it important to notify him that they had disobeyed a direct command by travelling to this star system. He stared at the message, occasionally glancing across at Adra to make sure her attention was still directed elsewhere, and contemplated his next action. Eventually, he plucked up the courage to ask the question that his better senses told him not to ask.

"Provost, if I may interrupt," Lux began, being careful to remain respectful, but also trying to convey a sense of concern and urgency, "Warfare Command are requesting an update on when we will arrive at the rendezvous co-ordinates for our escort duty."

Adra stepped back from the science console and turned to face Lux. She studied the Adjutant for a moment; he looked tense and anxious, despite obvious efforts to appear at ease. "I will respond to Warfare Command directly.

"Yes, Provost," Lux answered, and then uneasily he added, "If I may ask, Provost Adra, why..."

"You may *not* ask," Adra cut in sharply. "Warfare Command is not your concern. You need only concern yourself with my orders, is that clear?"

"Apologies, Provost," said Lux, bowing his head respectfully, despite at that moment feeling a swell of resentment towards his commander.

Adra moved back onto her command platform and saw another incoming message alert flash up on one of the halo of screens. She motioned the display towards her, causing it to swing down, and was relieved to discover that it was not another bothersome message from Warfare Command, but an update to the regular information bulletin that was circulated to all ships. She read the new entry, 'Advisory: Disturbance at Way Station G-7J00.' It was a regular security advisory, Adra realized, and something that one of the smaller ships would typically deal with. She was about to dismiss the alert and wave off the screen, when she had a sudden urge to check the location of this Way Station. She brought up the star chart on the screen and centered in on the location of the alert. The chart was sub-dived into a vast three-dimensional grid of cubes, each of which contained a super-luminal transceiver at the center. Adra added their own location to the chart and watched keenly as the image pulled back to indicate their relative positions. Her scowl deepened; Way Station G-7J00 was only a few standard jumps from their current location – practically neighbors in galactic terms – and close enough that her War Frigate could perhaps traverse the distance in one, if she pushed the jump boundary beyond the safe tolerances. Adra did not relish the prospect of what such a long jump would do to her body, but she felt in her bones that these events were all somehow connected. Then she had a thought, and switched her screen to show a status readout of the CoreNet. She narrowed in on the super-luminal transceiver that encompassed Way Station G-7J00 and then ran an analysis of the signal patterns during the time the disturbance had taken place. She watched the patterns keenly and then she saw it and paused the display. There had been a spike in the CoreNet shortly before the incident had taken place, and the readings closely matched the anomaly they had tracked to this star system. Adra did not believe in random coincidences; in her mind these events were connected.

Adra switched back to the bulletin screen and highlighted the alert; two options appeared, 'Respond' and 'Ignore'. Without hesitation she tapped 'Respond'. She then closed the bulletin and star map and opened the message from Warfare Command that Lux had been so anxious about, and drafted a short reply. 'Experienced technical difficulties. Unable to make rendezvous. Request Warfare Command to re-assign. Headed to Way Station G-7J00 for diagnostic.' She sent the message and locked all further communications from Warfare Command to her eyes only, before dismissing the screen back to its perch high above the command platform with a flourish of her hand.

She noticed that Lux was still attentively watching her and patiently waiting for further instructions, hands pressed by his side, neck and shoulders tensed, and restless eyes betraying his discomfort at being kept ignorant of Adra's true intentions. But she was unconcerned about Lux; he would perform his duty or she would remove him, as was the way of things. Adra's status would afford her some considerable leeway from Warfare Command, and she knew it. But she also knew that the tether would not extend indefinitely; she would need to find something more concrete to take back to her superiors soon, or the next ship that would be hunted down would be hers. She pressed her hands behind her back and peered down at Lux from her elevated position on the command platform.

"Prepare the ship to jump." She said, calmly.

Lux nodded, and moved between the two pilot simulants, tapping the primary pilot sharply on the shoulder so that it was primed to receive the order. "What is our destination, Provost?"

"Way Station G-7J00."

Lux glanced down at the navigational system and saw that the co-ordinates had already been relayed, along with the jump pattern. He saw the length of the blind jump that Adra had inputted and felt his stomach lighten. He glanced back, ready to question the order, but then thought better of it. He was on a razor's edge with Adra already, and given the choice between the consequences of insubordination and the mental and physical punishment of such a dangerous jump, he chose the lesser of two evils.

The whine of the jump engines began to build to a crescendo. "Co-ordinates locked in, Provost Adra. We are ready to jump."

"Execute."

Lux simply nodded and then faced forwards

again. He tapped the primary pilot simulant with the back of his hand to start the jump countdown and then slid his fingers through the framework of the chairs to either side, grasping them so tightly that the metal groaned and under the pressure of his vice-like grip. Then the War Frigate jumped and the mental and physical torment began again.

SEVEN

The communications console bleeped an alert for another incoming message and this time Taylor checked the screen and read the text out loud, "Corvette Contingency One, you are cleared to jump. Validate jump co-ordinates or clear the line."

"Sounds like they're getting impatient," said Sonner, while she tapped out a response. Taylor read the message as she entered it, 'Contingency One experiencing technical difficulties. Request to dock for repairs.'

"Are you sure about this?" asked Taylor, still struggling to believe Sonner really intended to board the Hedalt station. "I mean, unless you've forgotten, you're a human and I'm a simulant. We're hardly inconspicuous."

The response from the space station flashed up on the screen, 'Acknowledged, Contingency One. Transmitting docking pattern.'

"See? We're already half-way there," said Sonner, pointing triumphantly to the message on the screen. "Come on, Captain, how about some optimism?"

Taylor winced. *Optimism, optimism, optimism...* he repeated over and over in his mind. *Pull it together, Taylor.* He hated that he had become the one to point out problems and shoot down ideas, rather than the one to courageously solve them. He glanced over to where Blake used to sit at the tactical console, and remembered again how he'd always moaned and complained and tried to drag the others down. He didn't want to become like him.

"Sorry, Commander," Taylor sighed, "perhaps you can find out a way to reverse the polarity of my simulant body."

Sonner raised an eyebrow, "Reverse the polarity?"

"You know, negative to positive? Come on, that's an engineering joke!"

Sonner shook her head and pointed to the pilot's console, "I'd stick to flying if I were you, Captain."

Taylor rolled his silver eyes and returned to his seat, before loading the docking pattern that the station had transmitted. "Without wanting to sound glass-half-empty again, exactly how do you propose that we move around on this station without attracting attention? I haven't been alive all that long, and don't fancy getting myself killed."

Sonner shut down the mission ops console and moved beside Taylor, resting on the back of the pilot's chair. "Hedalt don't look much different to humans, remember?" she said, undeterred. "I'll just need some sort of appropriate clothing, and perhaps a bit of make-up to make my skin look even grayer than it already is. Though I must admit, it's been a while since I've had to make myself look beautiful."

"You need to make yourself look alien, not beautiful," Taylor chipped in, "but what about me? I think I'm beyond a bit of mascara..."

"Judging from the scans of the station, there are already hundreds of simulants over there already. So just act all simulant-y and you'll be okay."

Taylor arched his neck back and looked up at Sonner, "Simulant-y?"

"You'll figure it out, Captain," said Sonner, slapping him on the shoulder. "Besides, there over two thousand Hedalt and simulants on that station and no-one is looking for us. We'll be fine."

Optimism... Taylor told himself again, before answering, "If you say so, but you'll have to do all the talking, because I don't speak 'Hedaltese' or whatever language it is they all speak."

"You do actually," replied Sonner cheerfully, "the language is programmed into that modified brain of yours. You already slip between the two languages without even realizing; it must all sound the same to you. I had to learn it the hard way."

"Really?" said Taylor, his simulant vocal box producing a perfect reproduction of incredulity. "Hell, is there anything else about me that I need to know?"

Sonner just winked and smiled, and Taylor almost took the bait, but decided not to rise on this occasion. They had other things to worry about, the most pressing of which was how to infiltrate an enemy space station. He returned his attention to the controls and lifted the pilot's viewport up to his eyes to start the docking process. Sonner, meanwhile, reached over him and punched a few commands into his console to relay a schematic layout of the space station onto the main viewport. Taylor peeked out from the side of the pilot's viewport to study the schematic. To his silver eyes it was just a nightmarish labyrinth of chaotically-connected spaces with no apparent logical order to any of it.

"Is that the station? It's like a damn rabbit warren."

"Great analogy, especially considering you've never actually seen a rabbit," said Sonner, with her usual verve. "I also managed to tap into a data feed from the station's central core; whoever runs this shit-hole of a space station obviously has the IQ of a carrot."

Taylor laughed, and then looked back into the pilot's viewport to more accurately position the Corvette over their designated docking platform. When the co-ordinates matched, he locked in their position and started the landing cycle, before shoving the pilot's viewport away and looking up at Sonner with an accurately-simulated quizzical expression. "Were you always so charming, Commander?"

Sonner back-handed Taylor in the ribs, but then regretted it, as his synthetic torso was actually constructed from some kind of composite alien alloy that was harder than titanium. "Ow, damn it, remind me not to do that again," she said, shaking her hand as if it had been stung by a wasp.

"You were talking about the data feed from the station?" Taylor said, smirking. Sometimes his simulant body had its benefits.

"Right..." Sonner placed her bruised hand back in her jacket pocket, but then she noticed that Taylor was still smirking. "And you can wipe that damn smile off your plastic face, Captain!" she added, though she was also struggling not to smile. Taylor waved his hand in front of his face like a mime artist wiping away one expression and replacing it with another, changing his smirk to a more stoic look. "Better..." said Sonner, still smiling. "As I was saying, I tapped into a data feed and found some useful information about the layout of this mess." Sonner pointed to one of the larger structures above the deck. "Anyone who is anyone will live in one of these towers; these are the upmarket districts, if you like. The penthouse suites of the rich and famous."

"The crooks more like..." said Taylor, cynically. "And I guess that means the rats live below deck, is that what you're saying?"

"Pretty much, yes. Black markets, disreputable establishments, smugglers... that's where we're likely to find what we need."

A solid thud resounded around the bridge as the Corvette touched down on the platform, which then opened up and swallowed the ship into the belly of the carrier-shaped space station.

"You take me to all the nicest places," said Taylor and Sonner smiled. She seemed to be enjoying herself. "You'd best go and slap on your alien face, because it seems that we've a heist to carry out..."

EIGHT

Air hissed around the seals of the cargo ramp as it lowered onto the inner landing deck of the Hedalt space station. Sonner stepped down first, with Taylor a few paces behind, far more cautiously and making a concerted effort to appear 'simulant-y'. The deck was bustling with activity and no-one paid them the slightest bit of attention, which was a relief to Taylor, as he'd half-expected to be shot the moment the ramp was lowered.

Sonner stepped out onto the deck and then glanced back at Taylor to make sure he hadn't chickened out and slipped back into the hold. Using the ship's workshop, and assisted by the small army of manufacturing and repair drones that Sonner had brought with them from the Contingency base, she had managed to fabricate a

Hedalt uniform, based on data in the archives. Since this data was over three hundred years old, and conscious that fashions may have changed somewhat since then, she had created a version of a Hedalt soldier's long black coat that had a hood, which she wore up, casting her face into shadow. Anyone that did look Sonner in the eyes would see the grayish face of a Hedalt soldier staring back at them, thanks to a form of body paint that the industrious drones had also fabricated.

"You look like you're going to a goth motocross convention or something," said Taylor as he reached her side and saw Sonner for the first time under the murkier lighting of the space station. She certainly cut an imposing figure. He had provided input on the design of the armor-like uniform from memory, since he had seen a Hedalt soldier recently, during his jaunt inside the Fabric.

"Well, you look like my simulant slave," Sonner hit back. "Do you want to know why?" She didn't wait for Taylor to answer before adding, "because that's what you are, at least while we're here. Now, act simulant-y and stay quiet; I doubt anyone in this backwater hell-hole has seen an advanced simulant like you before, and the last thing we need to do is to attract any unwanted attention."

"Aye, aye Commander Sarah Sonner," said Taylor, quietly enough that no-one other than Sonner could hear. Then he spotted someone approaching; a Hedalt male dressed in dirty green overalls that seemed slightly too small for him, revealing a portly gut and tree-trunk legs. He nudged Sonner to get her attention, before acting simulant-y again. Sonner took the hint and straightened her posture, projecting to her full height, which was actually a little taller than Taylor. He hadn't realized how much she'd been slouching until then.

"Corvette Contingency One?" the Hedalt queried, ambling closer without really paying attention to either one of them, "Declare your cargo and pay the docking toll..." then the male looked up mid-sentence and was struck dumb. His grey face paled and he backed away, bowing his head so that he was looking at Sonner's boots. "Apologies, Vice-Provost, I did not realize that this was a Warfare Command vessel. I had not been informed of your arrival."

Sonner glanced back at Taylor, wide-eyed, as if looking for his advice on how to respond, but Taylor simply mimicked her startled rabbit expression and shrugged, unhelpfully. Sonner shot him a dirty look and turned back to the Hedalt male, who had missed the exchange because he was still gazing at Sonner's feet. "We are on a secret mission," began Sonner, and then she winced, realizing how hammy that sounded. She had also put on a sort of mock aristocratic-sounding accent, as if she was playing a fantasy role-playing game, and her character was a noble warrior or knight. Despite the precariousness of their situation, Taylor almost burst out laughing. "Our presence on this station must remain unknown," Sonner continued, in the same put-on voice.

"Of course, Vice-Provost, I will see to it, and have your ship fueled," the male continued. "I am the Sub-Deck Chief for this dock; Mallor is my name." Mallor nervously lifted his head, hoping that he had placated the figure he believed to be a senior Hedalt officer; he saw Taylor clearly for the first time and did a double-take. "Is that a Hunter simulant?" he said, sounding like a child who had just spied a favorite toy in a shop window. "I have never seen one out of stasis!"

"Never mind my simulant," Sonner replied, with a waft of her hand, throwing herself into the role. Taylor scowled, affronted by Sonner's reference to him, as if he was her slave, but decided it was best to remain quiet and 'simulant-y'. "We are looking for equipment, likely black market contraband. Where on this station would I find this?"

Mallor immediately tensed up and bowed his head again, before stuttering a response, "I... I know of no such contraband..."

"All information will be treated in confidence,"

Sonner said, worried that she had already pushed too far. Then she felt a tap on her shoulder, and glanced back to see Taylor doing a mime, rubbing his thumb and fingers together. Sonner scowled at him, shaking her head.

"Reward..." Taylor said as quietly as possible, and Sonner suddenly got his gist.

"And you will be rewarded for your..." Sonner had to think what the Hedalt would value most, other than the annihilation of another species, and went with, "loyalty." This seemed to work and Mallor appeared to relax a little.

"Thank you, Vice-Provost. If I was to know of such a place – and I do not of course, but if I did – I would suggest asking at the Freighter Guild, on sub-level seven. You can't miss it, it's where most people on that level will be headed."

"Very good, Sub-Deck Chief Mallor, you may leave," commanded Sonner, with a knightly wave of her hand, as if dismissing him from court. If Taylor had still had a tongue, he would have needed to bite it to prevent laughter, but as it was he buried his face in his arm and let out a muffled snort. Sonner back-heeled him in the shin, though it was like kicking a steel post. The kick did the trick, though, and Taylor fell silent again, though it wasn't necessary as Mallor had already embraced the opportunity to scurry away.

Sonner turned back to Taylor after she was sure

that Mallor had gone and that no-one else was approaching them. "See, I told you this was going to work, no thanks to you."

"Next time, warn me before you go all thespian like that," said Taylor, smirking. "You sounded like the damn Lady of the Lake."

"The Lady of what?" said Sonner, but then just waved her hand dismissively at him, still in character. "You know what? I honestly don't care. Come on, we need to find sub-level seven."

"Lead the way, oh mighty Vice-Provost..." Taylor replied theatrically, and Sonner jabbed him in the shins again.

NINE

The elevator whirred and groaned as it descended deeper into the sub levels of the massive station, like a lump of food being swallowed by a gigantic space beast. It had taken Taylor and Sonner fifteen minutes to find a way down to sub-level seven, and in that time they had drawn sideways glances from almost everyone they had passed. Most of the population was as terrified at the sight of Sonner as Mallor had been, while the few who weren't afraid looked like they would as soon slit their throats and rob them as say 'hello'. On this front, Taylor had an advantage, in that slitting his throat would have no effect whatsoever.

Taylor had noticed a pattern to the attention they would get; first, they would look at Taylor and double-take in a way that suggested he was an uncommon sight. Certainly, all the other simulants they'd seen so far on the station were identical and far more mannequin-like in appearance. This double-take would normally be followed by what could only be described as a contemptuous glower, though it seemed to Taylor that contemptuous was the Hedalt's default expression, so he hadn't read too much into it. Next they would look at Sonner, still mostly shrouded by her long, hooded cloak, as if sizing her up for a fight, but the instant her armored uniform became apparent, they would look away and give her as wide a berth as possible, without it appearing too obvious. Sonner had noticed the beneficial – though unintended – consequence of her choice of outfit too, and had taken any opportunity to gloat to Taylor about how well her plan was working out.

The elevator eventually stopped at sub-level seven and the doors juddered open, grinding into their housing in a way that suggested the contraption hadn't been properly maintained for some time. The two other Hedalt who were in the elevator hung back reverently and waited for Sonner to leave first, but then brushed past Taylor as if he wasn't even there.

"Something tells me that they don't have much love for simulants," said Taylor, once the two Hedalt were out of earshot.

"Oh, I'm sure they have a lot of love for them, or more specifically for what they do," Sonner answered, "it's just that they don't have any respect for them. To the Hedalt, you're nothing more than a toaster."

"That's just great," sighed Taylor, "this is going to be a fun trip then."

"Don't worry, Captain, I'll protect you," said Sonner, and though he couldn't see properly because of the hood, he knew she was smirking.

They continued on for a few minutes, following the flow of the crowd as the deck hand, Mallor, had suggested. Sub-level seven was even busier than the top deck, Taylor observed, and making progress through the mass of Hedalt bodies would have been slow going had it not been for Sonner's presence cutting a path through them, like Moses parting the waves.

"There..." said Sonner, pointing to what looked like a wide store front about fifty meters ahead. It seemed to occupy almost an entire side of the cavernous lower deck and was certainly the focus of the activity on the sub-level, with a constant stream of Hedalt flowing in and out of the large, arched entrance. "I reckon that must be our place; this Freighter Guild that Mallor talked about."

Taylor could already clearly see inside through the arched doorway of the establishment thanks to his hawk-like simulant eyes, and he instantly recognized it for what it was. Apparently, a dive bar was a dive bar, no matter whether you were in some jerkwater town, or a decrepit space station fifteen thousand light years from Earth.

"Well, you said we needed to find somewhere disreputable," said Taylor, "and that place certainly fits the bill. What's your plan?"

Sonner thought for a moment, and then indicated to her intimidating uniform. "Mallor referred to me as Vice-Provost. I know that Provost was an esteemed rank in the Hedalt military hierarchy, and this suggests nothing has changed on that front."

"Everyone gives you a wide birth, that's for sure," agreed Taylor. "But if you are a senior and respected figure of authority, we can hardly waltz through the door of this dive and barter for black market tech, like a couple of low-life scoundrels."

"That's true, but what if we're not looking to buy?" said Sonner, with a sparkle in her eyes. "What if I'm in there to apprehend the bad guys who sell it?"

Taylor's synthetic lips curled into a smile and he nodded, "Not bad, Commander. We can shake the place down, find what we need, and confiscate the illicit goods."

"Got it in one, Captain."

"But, this all assumes the bad guys we need are actually in there and selling that sort of black market tech." Taylor was conscious to phrase it more as a question, so as not to come across as negative again.

Sonner peered back at the entrance to the Freighter Guild; it was partially hidden in shadow, with a mix of boarded up and blacked out windows to prevent anyone from seeing too much of the interior from outside, and in general it looked like the sort of place any sensible person would cross the street to avoid. Taylor's description of it as a dive was on the money. "Just look at that place, Captain," she said, nodding towards it. "Nothing good goes on in a place like that. Besides, where there's opportunity, there's crime, and I'm sure this sort of off-grid space station offers plenty of opportunities for a certain kind of person."

Taylor found himself agreeing; from the reaction of everyone on the station to Sonner, it seemed clear that the Hedalt military rarely reached out this far, and though he assumed there must be some sort of law and order on the station, he'd seen no evidence of it so far. This was exactly the sort of place that would thrive on a trade in contraband. "Okay then, Vice Provost Sonner, let's go shopping."

Taylor followed behind Sonner as she walked towards the arched doorway to the Freighter Guild, clearing a path for them like a minesweeper. She then flung open the giant glass doors in a manner that Taylor considered a little over-dramatic, and stepped inside. As he followed Sonner into the dingy, musty-smelling interior, it was clear that their flamboyant entrance had gone unnoticed. The interior space was arranged around a large, oval-shaped central island, which Taylor assumed was the equivalent of the bar, and as with any good bar, there were several drunk-looking figures slumped up against it. Lining the walls around the outside of the Freighter Guild were a mix of deep alcoves and other nooks and crannies, which seemed perfect for conducting affairs of the sort that you'd want to keep hidden from the prying eyes and ears of law enforcers. Sonner glanced back at Taylor and raised her eyebrows, obviously thinking the same as him. *What a dump.*

Sonner lead them further into the room and towards the central island, eventually stopping at an empty, standing-height table that had a couple of plates of half-eaten food on it. The surface was damp and sticky with a pungent-smelling slime that Taylor had no desire to identify.

"Any ideas what we do next?" asked Sonner, who was scrunching up her nose, Taylor assumed because of the smell. Taylor could smell it too, though without a stomach to turn, the stench didn't offend him nearly as much as it clearly did Sonner.

"If you want to find out anything in a bar, talk to the barman," offered Taylor, nodding towards the central island.

"Isn't that a little clichéd?"

"It's only a cliché because it's true," Taylor replied, with an air of smugness. "You go, I'll wait here and make sure someone doesn't steal our table."

Sonner glanced at the festering detritus in front of her and scrunched her nose up again, but then nodded and headed off towards the bar.

"Hey!"

The shout came from behind Taylor, deeper into the room. He turned to see what the shout was about, but didn't see any signs of commotion or anything unusual, so he turned back to keep watch over Sonner as she tried to grab the attention of a Hedalt female standing in the central island. The next thing Taylor knew, a hand was grabbing the top of his shoulder and it twisted him a hundred and eighty degrees.

"Hey, freak, I'm talking to you!" Taylor was suddenly confronted with a robust-looking Hedalt male with a heavy brow and perfectly bald head that shone like a marble. He looked like he was carrying a spare fifty pounds, but this only emphasized his already immense stature, which made a pro-wrestler look ordinary. At least thirty centimeters taller than Taylor, he was dressed in a dark green uniform with a patch on the right breast pocket that included the same emblem that was emblazoned on the exterior facade. "Walking brains like you aren't allowed in here; are you malfunctioning or something?"

Taylor was completely thrown and had no clue how best to respond. Did regular simulants speak? If they did, was their speech normal, or more akin to a bad voice synthesizer? He tried to remember how the other simulants he'd seen while in the Fabric looked and acted, and then remembered Sonner telling him to act all 'simulant-y', but all of it added up to a big fat nothing. Instead, he just stood in the shadow of the hulking creature, struck dumb.

There was a shout from somewhere else across the room, "Hey, that thing seems to have as much brains as you do!", which was followed by a ripple of laughter that seeped out from the many nooks and crannies.

"Shut your face!" the large Hedalt called back, but his attention was still focused on Taylor. "Okay, freak, out you go," he continued, grabbing Taylor by the arm and attempting to pull him towards the archway. Instinctively, Taylor's self-defense training kicked in, and he grabbed the Hedalt's wrist, wrenching it back and practically lifting the giant man off the ground, forgetting his inhuman strength, which was one of the few beneficial side-effects of his simulant form. The Hedalt cried out in pain, suspended on the very tips of his toes, and suddenly the room fell silent. Chairs screeched across the hard floor and boots shuffled in the alcoves as every Hedalt in the Freighter Guild rose sharply to their feet. Taylor could see many of them arming themselves with whatever came soonest to hand; some had knives, while others smashed chairs or stools to create improvised clubs. Taylor scanned the room with his keen simulant eyes and saw two Hedalt drawing compact sidearms that had previously been concealed inside their long coats. His human fight or flight response kicked in, though his simulant body remained unmoved by the sudden burst of emotion. He was ready to throw the man down and make a dash for the door when another voice cut through the tension like a plasma shard.

"What is the meaning of this?" cried Sonner, sounding genuinely authoritative. Unlike her earlier, slightly comedic attempts at mimicking a Hedalt officer, this was the real Sonner coming through, and Taylor was both impressed and intimidated by her ferocity and instant command of the room.

"Vice... Provost..." the large Hedalt answered, still partially suspended by his wrist and fighting against the agony that gripped his body, "I did... not know... you were here."

Sonner pointed a needle-straight finger towards the floor, indicating to Taylor in no uncertain terms that he should put the Hedalt down, which he did straight away. He then took a long pace back, grateful of the intervention. The large Hedalt shook his arm and then cradled it in front of his enormous chest.

"Apologies, Vice Provost, I assume this is yours?" the large Hedalt continued, briefly glancing over to Taylor. His tone was courteous, but not fearful like the others they had dealt with.

"Yes," replied Sonner, who then noticed that the entire room was still on its feet, as if an old-fashioned bar fight was about to erupt at any moment. "The rest of you, get back to your business!" she shouted towards the center of the throng, aiming the command at no-one in particular, and to Taylor's astonishment, they all did as ordered. It was like a scene out of an ancient western, where the whole saloon would go quiet when the sheriff marched in, but then just carried on drinking and playing poker when it became clear a gunfight was not on the cards.

"Simulants are not permitted in the guild, Vice Provost," the large Hedalt continued, "even Warfare Command honors that agreement." Taylor was surprised, and even a little impressed with how this Hedalt was handling himself; acting respectfully, but also not kowtowing to Sonner. "I am Guild Master Goker, the master of this franchise. And you are Vice Provost...?"

Sonner didn't respond to Goker's request for her name, mainly because she had no idea what Hedalt female names sounded like, and her synapses were firing on overtime just trying to improvise her way through the conversation without slipping up.

"I do not need an apology," Sonner said, sticking with a stern, spiky tone, "this is a matter of utmost urgency. Assist me and I will be on my way quickly."

Goker's large eyes narrowed slightly and he moved closer, anxiously looking to either side to check if anyone was close to enough to overhear him. When he was satisfied no-one was, he lowered his voice to a near whisper and said, "The guild is always happy to assist Warfare Command."

"I am looking to acquire a CoreNet transceiver. One that cannot be traced," Sonner said, also keeping her voice low so that she could not be overheard. Taylor realized that his simulant ears were just as keen as his eyes, because he heard every word clearly, and he also heard Goker swallow hard at Sonner's request. The Guild Master's eyes darted into the various dark corners of the room, again making sure there were no eavesdroppers. Taylor could even hear his massive heart thumping harder.

"I have no interest in you or this guild," Sonner added, continuing to improvise on the spot, "but if you can assist in this urgent matter then Warfare Command will be grateful. To you, personally."

Goker seemed to consider this for a moment, and then sighed, "I told them not to push those things through here, but it wasn't worth me getting killed over," he began. "We're a long way from the home world, Vice Provost. We don't see your sort out here much, and the station's security forces are a worse band of lowlifes than the scum in here."

"Who do you mean?" said Sonner, fighting hard to mask her excitement.

"Racketeers," growled Goker. "They've moved three unregistered transceivers through here recently, and I know they have at least one more. I told them to take it somewhere else, but had a knife pressed to my throat for my trouble." He then pointed a thick finger to a thin scar along the side of his neck that looked to be from a recently-healed wound.

"They are in here? Now?" asked Sonner, and Goker nodded. Sonner glanced at Taylor and he nodded back; confronting a criminal gang in a room that was likely packed full of villains and ne'er-do-wells was a big risk, but the payoff was even bigger, if they could pull it off. They didn't have a choice; without a transceiver, their chances of reaching the second Contingency base were slim to none. "Where?" asked Sonner, and Goker aimed his fat finger at the far corner of the room, towards one of the larger alcoves that was tucked out of view.

"The one you want has a scar down the side of her face, from temple to chin," said Goker, nervously stroking his scar. "Her name is Rheyda and she's a nasty piece of work. If I were you, I'd go in armed. Just try not to make a mess, if you can help it."

Sonner almost thanked Goker, but then thought better of it; from the unfavorable way he'd spoken about Warfare Command, Sonner didn't get the impression that it was an organization whose members minded their Ps and Qs, especially with those in the lower echelons of society. Instead, she nodded formally and cocked an eyebrow at Taylor, who understood her intention and followed her towards the alcove.

"I wish I'd brought a damn weapon with me," said Sonner under her breath.

"You did," replied Taylor, "you brought me."

TEN

Together, Sonner and Taylor moved deeper into the bowels of the Freighter Guild and stood in the entrance to the alcove Goker had indicated. Inside were three Hedalt; a female and two males. They each took one look at Sonner's distinctive armored uniform and sprang to their feet, reaching inside their coats with practiced speed and efficiency, but Taylor's enhanced senses were quicker still. He darted forwards and grabbed a thick dark-tinted drinking glass from the table, flinging it into the face of the closest male and knocking him flat, as if he'd been hit with a cannon ball.

Sonner too had moved quickly, anticipating resistance, and had caught the arm of the second male, before he was able to pull out whatever weapon was concealed inside his coat. She then sliced the palm of her hand into the Hedalt's throat, before shifting position and using her weight to slam his oxygen-starved face into the wall of the alcove. She heard the crunch of bone and cartilage, and when she released her hold, the male fell like a stone.

The Hedalt female was more agile, and vaulted the table, kicking Sonner in the back, before charging into Taylor. She must have expected her momentum to topple him like a bowling pin, but Taylor merely stumbled back a few paces and held firm. Grasping her shoulder and crying out with pain, the female then pulled a knife from inside her coat and thrust it towards him, but Taylor deflected the attack with his forearm, which was accompanied by a sharp crack as the Hedalt female's wrist was snapped by the force of Taylor's block. The knife dropped out of her hand and embedded into Taylor's foot, but his simulant body detected no pain and so he continued on, oblivious to the injury, grabbing the female by her jacket and lifting her off her feet as if she weighed nothing.

The female peered into Taylor's silver eyes, her face a conflicted mess of agony and bewilderment, and it was then that Taylor got a good look at the long scar reaching down from her temple to the line of her chin – the scar that told him this was

Rheyda, the racketeer they were searching for. He tossed her back into the alcove as if she were a sack of wool and then blocked the exit like a doorman, while Sonner rounded on Rheyda, burning white-hot with anger.

"Who are you?" Rheyda shouted, cradling her wrist. "I've done nothing wrong!"

"I'm the last person you'll see, unless you do as I say," Sonner rasped, with such fire and venom that Taylor couldn't be certain if it was an act, or a serious threat. Sonner may have been snarky and spiky, but she had always been in control of her emotions; now she looked like a woman on the verge of losing control and giving over to an instinct for vengeance.

"You can't threaten me, not in the Guild. Even you respect those rules!" Rheyda blurted out, shrinking away from Sonner, who continued to advance on her, fists clenched, before grabbing the collar of Rheyda's jacket and pulling back her arm, ready to strike.

"I don't care about your idiotic guild," she snarled, "Give me what I want, or I'll beat it from you!"

Taylor felt he had to intervene somehow, but without making it obvious that he was no ordinary simulant. He took a step forward and Sonner's tongue-in-cheek advice came back to mind... *Act 'simulant-y'*

"Vice-Provost, you have a communication from the ship," Taylor said, trying to sound vaguely artificial and robotic. He had no idea if that was how simulants spoke, or even if they spoke.

Sonner's fist dropped slightly and she glanced over at Taylor, forehead scrunched tightly. "What? What communication?" she said, and then she saw the smooth, slightly shiny simulant skin on Taylor's forehead wrinkle, as his eyes widened in an attempt to subtly convey his trepidation at what Sonner was doing. The interjection was enough to break Sonner out of her near-frenzy and she took a step back, unclenching her fist. "Never mind, I'll deal with it later," she added, going along with Taylor, who simply nodded and stepped back.

Rheyda looked relieved, but also confused, "How does your thing speak? I never heard one speak before."

"That's none of your concern, Rheyda," Sonner replied, stressing the name, as if she was revealing her secret identity. Rheyda looked suitably alarmed that she was already known to the woman she saw as a Vice Provost.

"How do you know me? I've done nothing!" Rheyda protested, but Sonner just continued her interrogation.

"You are a racketeer who has been smuggling unregistered starship transceivers through this station," Sonner stated, calm authority replacing resentful fury. Rheyda tried to hide it, but it was clear from her reaction that Sonner had spoken the truth. "Give the remaining unit to me, and I may overlook your transgression, on one condition."

Rheyda seemed astonished by the offer, "What? You mean, you'll let me go free?"

"Yes, providing you speak of this to no-one, not even others from Warfare Command," said Sonner, flatly. "My presence here is classified. If you break this condition, I will know, and you will not wake up the following morning. Do you understand?"

Again, Taylor was impressed at how convincing Sonner sounded, so much so that he almost believed she had the ability to assassinate this female from half-way across the galaxy, like some kind of pan-galactic secret agent. Rheyda seemed to be equally convinced; they may have been a different species, but fear shimmered behind the eyes of the Hedalt in the same way it did in humans.

"If it means you'll leave me alone, I'll have it transferred," Rheyda said, growing emboldened by Sonner's unexpected promise not to kill her. Like Goker, she displayed none of the respect or fearful reverence of Sonner's perceived rank or uniform as others on the station had done, "Yours is the Corvette docked in section seven, right?"

Sonner frowned, and was about to ask how

Rheyda knew this, but the racketeer answered the question without being promoted. "What, do you really think a Vice Provost lands on a station like this every day?" Rheyda added, talking to Sonner as if she was an imbecile. "Everyone in this room knew you'd landed even before you did."

Taylor very nearly broke his simulant cover to call out to Sonner, but just managed to hold off and continue his simulant-y act. He wanted to point out that they hadn't docked in section seven, meaning that Rheyda was referring to another Corvette. Then Taylor realized something and he felt a buzz of excitement whizz around his brain. *Corvette... Does she mean another Hunter Corvette?* If there was a Hunter Corvette docked at the station then chances are it also contained members of his crew, or at least other simulant recreations of them. Taylor was desperate to tell Sonner his theory, but he first needed to make sure the racketeer sent the contraband to the correct ship, otherwise they wouldn't be leaving the station any time soon. He was unwilling to speak up again, given that Rheyda had said simulants typically don't speak, but he saw no other option.

"Vice Provost, that is not the correct docking platform," said Taylor, again putting on a robotic sounding voice.

Sonner scowled at him and then the penny dropped. She turned back to Rheyda, "Apparently, not everyone in the room is as smart as they think they are..." she said, enjoying correcting the cocky racketeer. "Have it transferred to a Corvette designated as Contingency One. Arrange it with Sub-Deck Chief Mallor."

"Whatever you say," muttered Rheyda.

"If a word of this leaks out of this alcove, you'll wish I had killed you here," Sonner added, sounding like she really meant it.

This time Rheyda bit her tongue and just nodded. Sonner scowled back at her for another second or two and then turned, stepping over the unconscious body of the Hedalt she had smashed into the wall earlier, and stormed out of the alcove. Taylor followed, first making sure that Rheyda didn't try to literally stab them in the back, but once he was clear of the alcove and out of earshot of anyone else, he caught up with Sonner and got her attention.

"What's up?" Sonner said, turning to face him. She still looked and sounded furious.

"Are you okay? I thought you were about to actually murder her for a moment," Taylor asked.

"It's more than she deserves. It more than any of them deserve," spat Sonner, causing Taylor to recoil slightly, but then Sonner's anger seemed to ebb, like a pan suddenly taken off the boil. "But, thanks for reining me in back there."

"Hey, for what it's worth, I understand your

anger," said Taylor. "I'm almost glad I don't have blood anymore, because I'm sure mine would have boiled, just like yours did. But I know one thing; we won't beat them by becoming them."

Sonner nodded and then cocked an eyebrow, "Is that why you dragged me back, for a little pep talk?"

"No, but you're welcome anyway..." Taylor was getting used to Sonner's prickliness, and actually welcomed it, because it meant he knew she was acting normally again. "Rheyda said there was another Corvette docked here," said Taylor getting straight to the point. "That could be another ship like mine."

Sonner immediately caught his gist and tipped her head back, closing her eyes, "Captain, now is not the time. We need that transceiver installed as a matter of urgency. Everything depends on us being able to jump along the threads of the Fabric."

"I know that, but if there's a Hunter Corvette here, now, we may never get a better chance," Taylor replied. "You've seen how sloppily everything around here is run; if the deck security is anything like as bad as it is for the rest of the station, we could be in and out before anyone knows any different."

"Isn't one heist in a day enough for you?" Sonner replied, ladling in an extra dollop of snark. "It's too risky, Taylor."

Taylor's silver eyes almost popped out of his head, "Too risky? After what we just pulled?"

Sonner tried to answer back, but Taylor had a point, and instead she faltered and stammered, mouth slightly agape.

"You owe me Commander, remember?" Taylor pressed on, "There may never be a chance as good as this. I owe it to my crew, and frankly so do you."

Sonner let out a frustrated growl and stared down at the floor, hands on hips. Then she noticed the knife that was still impaled through the top of Taylor's boot. "You have a knife stuck in your foot, did you know that?"

"Stop changing the subject."

Sonner bent down and pulled the knife out, before waggling it in front of Taylor's nose like an angry finger, "Okay, okay, damn it, but if we get killed in the process then I'm going to shove this knife up your..."

Just at that moment Guild Master Goker plodded towards them, mercifully causing Sonner to cut her sentence short, though Taylor had a fairly good idea how it would have ended.

"Thanks for not making too much of a mess," said Goker, clearly trying to be funny, but coming across as slightly passive-aggressive. "I take it our arrangement still holds, then? You'll leave me out of this?"

"You need not concern yourself, Guild Master

Goker, providing you remain discreet."

"I will be more discreet than your simulant here," said Goker, glaring at Taylor as if he was muck on the sole of his boot. "Thankfully, the other simulants like him stay in stasis while their ships are docked for refueling and repairs. The dumb automaton ones are bad enough, but at least they stay silent. Likely, if it wasn't for your presence, Vice Provost, this thing would have been torn limb-from-limb, and nailed to the wall in pieces by now."

Sonner felt like saying, 'I know how they feel', but resisted the temptation. Still, the Hedalt's vehement hatred of simulants was surprising, considering how many of them the Hedalt employed. "If you don't want to see my simulant here again then I suggest you speak of this to no-one," said Sonner. "Because next time, he will be even less discreet, understood?"

Goker sighed, "Understood, Vice Provost."

Sonner headed for the door with Taylor keeping pace by her side.

"Did you hear what he said?" whispered Taylor.

"I heard," Sonner replied. "If your other simulant friends are in stasis on that ship, then a quick smash and grab might just work..."

ELEVEN

Sonner knew that a Hunter Corvette docked on the station presented a good opportunity to recover other simulant members of Taylor's crew, but she still felt it was too much of a risk, and did her best to talk Taylor out of the idea. "Wait until we've found the second base and bolstered our numbers"... "I still don't even know if I can 'wake' them up the same as you"... "Right now, the Contingency consists of us two – if we're captured or killed, any hope of fighting back dies with us..." and so on, but Taylor was resolute, as she had fully expected him to be. Sonner actually admired Taylor's determination to rescue his former colleagues; in his position, she would do no less, even if the odds were against them, as they were now. But more than this, Taylor's dedication to his crew – his friends – proved that he was, at his core, still human.

Sonner was also not convinced that the racketeer had been correct about there being another Hunter Corvette docked at the station, perhaps just confusing it with their ship, but a brief conversation with Mallor confirmed that Rheyda had been telling the truth.

"Yes, Vice-Provost, there is a Hunter Corvette, docked over in section seven," said Mallor, with the same deference as earlier. "It's the first I've seen for many years. They usually dock by the security office, so that the station militia can watch over the ship and make sure no-one tries to raid it. The simulants are all in stasis, of course. In fact, your one here is the only one of these special units I've ever seen active."

Sonner's heart sank to the pit of her stomach, "Militia?"

"Yes, Vice Provost, the station's local militia," Mallor answered. "Mercenaries mainly, hired in to help the Constable; we're too out of the way to have a garrison from Warfare Command."

Sonner shot a glance at Taylor, but he appeared unconcerned by the news. Clearly, nothing short of the station self-destructing or being swallowed into a black hole was going to dissuade him from his intention to mount the rescue attempt.

"How many are stationed here?" Sonner asked,

trying to sound calm and indifferent, as if the question was just asked in passing.

"It varies; between fifty and a hundred," Mallor responded. "Hired guns only tend to hang around until they get a better offer. Or they get killed." Sonner clenched her teeth together. *Fifty to a hundred militia...* Even if they were hired guns with no loyalty or desire to be injured or killed in the line of duty, this was still ten times more than they could realistically hope to handle. She chose not to steal a look at Taylor again, and instead raise the elephant in the room with him once Mallor had gone. But there was still one piece of information she needed the compliant deck chief to provide. "Has the transceiver been placed on-board?" she asked, suddenly feeling that they may need to leave in a hurry.

"Yes, it was transferred over just before you arrived," Mallor said, "Do you need any assistance with it?"

"No, that will be all Sub-Deck Chief," said Sonner, firmly. Mallor took the cue to leave, bowing his head and backing off, before turning and scampering away. Sonner waited for a few moments, chewing the inside of her mouth, and then turned to Taylor.

"I know what you're going to say..." said Taylor, showing no sign of backing down.

"Even if there are only fifty militia stationed

near that Corvette, there's no chance of us getting those simulants out," said Sonner, "you have to accept that, surely?"

"I accept that we can't fight our way past fifty armed militia," Taylor answered, but the evasiveness of his response just wound Sonner up tighter.

"What does that mean? You accept we have to call it off, or you accept that it's a suicide mission, but you're going to do it anyway?"

"Neither," said Taylor, smoothly, "I have an idea..."

Sonner had never seen a simulant looking smug before and it simply made her want to slap the annoying smirk off his face. Instead, she just placed her hands on her hips while her eyes invited Taylor to regale her with his brilliant plan.

"You remember when I told you how I'd entered into the Fabric, during my sleep sequence," Taylor began, unable to hide his excitement, "and how when I was drawn onto the Hedalt ship they were able to 'attack' me?"

"I remember," said Sonner, suddenly curious, though her hands were still firmly pressed to her hips, "you said they were trying to purge a signal anomaly from the CoreNet, the anomaly being you, I assume. But so what? What's your point, Captain?"

"Well, if they're able to attack me while I'm

plugged into the Fabric, what if I can attack their systems too?" Taylor offered. "What if this anomaly I seem to create in the CoreNet can disrupt any system connected to it? If I could somehow get inside this station while I'm connected, I could maybe disrupt its systems and create a distraction."

Sonner scowled and started to chew the inside of her mouth again. She had expected Taylor's plan to be gung-ho and militaristic in nature, but his suggestion was rooted in science, even if it was a new and unexplored field of science, and this put it firmly in her wheelhouse. After a few silent seconds, she said, "I don't believe I'm saying this, but it might be possible. It's worth a try."

"Hang on, can you say that again, it sounded like you were agreeing with me?"

"Very funny, Captain, don't push it," said Sonner, pressing her lips together. "Just call it a moment of madness and let's move on, before I change my mind."

"I doubt it will be your last moment of madness, or mine," Taylor quipped.

"It certainly won't be yours, of that I'm certain," Sonner hit back, "but what the hell, if rescuing these other simulants means that I get someone other than your sorry ass to talk to, it's got to be worth a shot."

"Charming..."

"Just plug yourself in and get ready," said Sonner, starting to regret her decision already. "In the meantime, I'll set my little drone friends to work installing the transceiver, so that when this hair-brained scheme of yours goes south we can at least jump away to somewhere safe."

Taylor smiled. For some reason, he knew this plan was going to work. He didn't know how or why, but he felt a lingering connection to the Fabric, as if it were a phantom limb that he could still sense and manipulate, even now. Once he was inside the Fabric and through the starlight door, he was sure he'd be able to use this connection to infiltrate the CoreNet.

But that wasn't why he was smiling. Though Sonner went out of her way to be pricklier than a cactus, he could see that there was still a living, beating heart underneath her spiky exterior. She could have ordered him to give up this chance to rescue Satomi and the others, and Taylor would have grudgingly agreed, but she hadn't. She wanted to do the right thing, even if the right thing wasn't necessarily the smart thing, and he respected her all the more for it. He nodded towards her and said, "Aye, aye, Commander Sarah Sonner."

TWELVE

Taylor stood inside the translucent corridor in space with the starlight door directly ahead. It all looked exactly the same as it had before, except that this time Taylor felt somehow energized by the place, as if his brain was recharging and healing itself, the way organic bodies do during sleep. This side of the starlight door was serene and peaceful; the side that was still detached from the Fabric, but he knew that once he stepped through the opening and emerged onto the other side, he would once again be connected to the vast network of super-luminal transceivers, allowing him to travel practically anywhere in the galaxy. But he was also aware that this would expose his consciousness to the Hedalt. The last time he had entered the Fabric, he had barely managed to escape, before the Hedalt 'purge' overcame him. It was an experience he did not want to repeat, not least because the consequences of this purge were still unknown. Perhaps the purge would just force him to 'wake up' again, as if jolted out of sleep by a nightmare, but the more sinister possibility was the purge might break his mind, and kill him.

He took a deep breath and let it out, feeling the soothing effect on his nerves, which were back in full force, along with other physical emotions, while he was connected. "Here goes nothing..." he said out loud, and then boldly stepped through the starlight door.

Immediately, the space around him filled up with bright, translucent cubes, some appearing closer and some so far away that they looked like distant stars. Between them were the invisible wormholes that were known as threads; super-highways that allowed starships to travel immense distances, and that allowed Taylor to traverse the Fabric using only his mind. This time, however, he only needed to travel a few hundred meters to the inside of section seven of the haggard space station where his ship, with him on-board, was docked.

Okay, focus on the space station... Taylor said to himself, pressing his eyes shut. He still wasn't really sure how exactly it was that he traveled from one place to another, but picturing the end location seemed to help. *Docking section seven...*

Docking section seven... Docking section seven...

"Taylor, are you still there?"

Taylor froze. He kept his eyes shut and waited for the voice to speak again, half-convinced that he'd imagined it.

"Taylor, if you're there, please say so. It's dark. I don't want to be alone."

"Satomi?" replied Taylor, his voice wavering. "Satomi, can you hear me?" A hundred questions flooded into Taylor's mind, but the one that pushed its way to the front of his thoughts was whether this was the same Satomi he'd spoken to last time. The Satomi that seemed to be 'awake'.

"Yes, I can hear you, Taylor," said Satomi, "you just went quiet for a while, that's all. You had me worried."

Taylor tried to recall their last conversation, but so much had happened that events were blurring into one another. "Satomi, what's the last thing you remember me saying?"

"Remember? Taylor, it was only a few seconds ago," Satomi replied, sounding confused and anxious, "You asked me about my mission, and I told you I was scared. Then you went quiet."

A few seconds ago? Taylor thought. *For her, practically no time has passed. But how can that be?* Still too afraid to open his eyes, Taylor said out loud, "Satomi, do you know where you are? Can you tell me where you are?" There was a deathly pause, the same as the last time they had spoken, and Taylor held his breath. The silence endured. *No, not again! She's gone...*

"I... don't know. I mean, I'm not sure..." Satomi said, and Taylor exhaled, smiling broadly. "I remember being in so many places, but they all seem like half-forgotten dreams to me now. I think I'm on a moon, or maybe a space station. But I feel different in here, when I'm talking to you. Where are you?"

"Satomi, I don't know how to explain what this is; hell, I don't know myself," Taylor said, starting to rush his words, conscious that their connection could be broken again at any moment. "This place, where we're talking to each other now, it's inside the Fabric..."

"Taylor, you're not making any sense..."

"Please, just listen. You're not who you think you are. I'm not who you think I am. We're copies of the people we remember. Human minds in simulant bodies. I don't know if you can even understand what I'm saying, but somehow, I think you're like me, and deep down I think you know you're different too."

"What are you talking about, I'm Satomi Rose, and you're Taylor Ray!" Satomi replied, her voice shaky. "You're scaring me, Taylor, if this is one of your jokes, it's not funny."

"Don't worry about it now; all that matters is

that I can find you," said Taylor, "Hopefully, I'll be able to find you very soon, and then I'll explain everything. Until then, try to focus on where you are. Try to see it and remember it, so you can tell me the next time we talk like this."

"Why don't I remember anything outside of this place?" said Satomi, starting to sound frightened, almost panicked, "This is all so strange. It's like nothing is real, except you."

Taylor focused his mind and steadied his resolve. He understood how disorientating and upsetting it was to learn the truth, but maybe he could spare this copy of Satomi the pain of the rude awakening he had endured. "I am real, Satomi, and so are you. You are Satomi Rose in every way that matters. And I am Taylor Ray. Concentrate on where you are, and try to remember..." He could feel his connection to her slipping away, like a communications signal slowly drawing out of range, "Remember me, and I'll find you soon..."

Then there was silence again. Taylor opened his eyes and sighed deeply. When Satomi had slipped away after the first time they'd spoken inside the Fabric, it felt like he'd lost her all over again. But this time he knew only their connection had been lost. And this time he had a real chance to find her, because perhaps she was only a few hundred meters away, in stasis inside the Hunter Corvette on the very same space station. The odds of such an encounter given the enormity of the galaxy were astronomical, but perhaps the Fabric had connected them in more ways than one. Perhaps it had also drawn them back together.

Energized by his meeting with Satomi, he focused his mind again and tried to step out through the Fabric and into the festering guts of the space station. *Come on Taylor, concentrate...* he said to himself, urging his ethereal body to move. He tried to picture the hangar, but for some reason he couldn't recall the layout, despite having been there only minutes earlier. Instead, an image of Sonner flashed into his mind, dressed in her intimidating black armor, and suddenly he was moving, flying along an invisible thread towards a nearby cube, and seconds later he was standing inside a Corvette. But not just any Corvette; it was his own ship, and standing in front of him, in the workshop, was Sonner.

"Commander, can you hear me?" Taylor called out, but there was no answer. He moved closer and tried to place a hand on Sonner's shoulder to literally grab her attention, but his hand just cut through Sonner's body, as if she was a ghost. Sonner twitched and rubbed her ear as if there was water trapped inside, but then continued to work on whatever it was she was doing. As initially shocking as it had been to see his hand pass through solid matter, it gave Taylor an idea. If he could pass through Sonner as if she were merely a hologram then perhaps he could pass through the walls of the space station too.

Taylor looked around the workshop, taking mental photographs of it in an effort to use it as an anchor so that he could return here again in a hurry if needed. Then he looked again at Sonner and said, "Don't go anywhere, Commander, I'll be back soon," before walking towards the far end of the workshop, stepping a little more hesitantly as he got closer to the solid metal wall, before passing straight through it, through bulkheads and other empty compartments and eventually out into the hangar. He looked down and saw that he was floating above the deck, and instinctively reached back to try to grab onto the hull of the ship, before remembering that he wasn't really there; at least not in body.

How the hell do I get to this other ship? Taylor said to himself, and then he had another idea. The other ship was a Hunter Corvette, which in all likelihood was configured with the same layout as his. He stepped further away from his own vessel, walking in mid-air and then turned back to look at the scorpion-like hull, reminded of how much uglier it was than the elegant Nimrods of Earth Fleet. *Focus, Taylor, Focus... Find the other ship... Fly to the Hunter Corvette...* The hangar deck became a blur as he shot through the structure of the enormous space station, passing through walls and engineering spaces and the bodies of hundreds of Hedalt, forcing him to throw up his arms in an effort to shield his face; another dumb human instinct that was as ridiculous as it was pointless.

And then he stopped. For a moment his eyes were blurry, but as they came back into focus he saw the predatory shape of a Corvette-class cruiser parked on the deck, comfortably set away from all the other ships in the same section. Uniquely, compared to the other ships, it was guarded by two Hedalt males, which Taylor assumed to be members of the station's security militia. They wore heavy, dark blue uniforms, which were nothing like the ornate, armored get-ups that Sonner had worn. Whoever these soldiers were, they were not in the same class as the Provosts of Warfare Command, Taylor realized.

Directly behind the ship was a large, glass-fronted room, and inside Taylor could see more Hedalt also wearing these same, simple blue uniforms. Taylor could make out cell blocks in the back, filled with unscrupulous-looking sorts, some of whom were passed out, or maybe already dead. He was reminded of the untrustworthy-looking characters that he'd seen inside the Freighter Guild, and began to wonder if the word 'freighter' actually meant 'pirate'.

Okay, now what? said Taylor, anxiously. This

was alien territory in more ways than one; he was used to meticulously planning his missions and going by the book, rather than winging it on a hope and a prayer. But there was no tech manual or standard operating procedure for the situation he found himself in now, so he was writing the rules as he went along.

Taylor took a closer look at the hangar deck, which was smaller and also in a better state of repair than the one where their ship had landed. All around the perimeter were light strips and security cameras, some of which were broken or inoperative, and a host of luminous information panels and ad hoardings of almost every shape and size. He closed his eyes and tried to recall the sensation he'd felt when the Hedalt ship had initiated its purge. Not the pain, which was hard to forget since the Fabric was the only place he ever felt pain now, but the deeper sensation of energy surging through his body, as if he was conducting an electric charge. As he concentrated he could feel the same charge building inside him again, as if it were flowing from the strange, ethereal plane of existence he now occupied through some invisible conduit and into the world outside. He opened his eyes and turned his attention to the vibrant strip lights and ad hoardings surrounding the deck, and suddenly there was a tingling sensation, spreading from his head throughout his body. He could feel the energy of the station, but it was more than that; he could also hear it. At first it was just a jumble of nonsense, a sort of white noise, but soon he was able to pick out specific sounds and even individual voices. He overheard private conversations, arguments about bar tabs, complaints about slow refueling times, lovers' quarrels, structural data analyses, power grid readings, arrest reports... it was all there, he just had to tune into it, like an ancient analog radio dial. It was exhilarating, like being physically plugged into the chatter of the universe. And then Taylor realized exactly what he had tuned in to – it was the CoreNet. All forms of communication or surveillance were connected to the CoreNet, which meant that all of this information – a galaxy's worth of personal data – flowed through the Fabric. Whatever interfaced with the CoreNet was connected to Taylor in this space, and if he could receive information then maybe he could also transmit.

He turned his attention back to the glass-fronted constabulary building and tried to feel the power surging though the conduits inside. *Overload...* He urged, *Overload!...* A stabbing pain seared into his skull, taking him utterly by surprise, and he yelled. The cry was like a bolt of lightning striking out into the constabulary building, and a second later the glass-wall smashed and almost every light, computer console and power conduit inside erupted into sparks and flames. The damage seemed to ripple out, blowing up ad hoardings and conduits all along the deck.

There was immediate panic as uniformed militia and other station inhabitants bolted from the scene, followed moments later by the criminals who had been freed from incarceration after the power to their cell blocks failed. There was fighting, hand-to-hand and with improvised weapons grabbed from desks or torn from the helpless grasp of stunned militia.

Taylor watched in astonishment, the pain inside his head slowly subsiding. "Did I just do that?" he wondered out loud, and then shook his head again, annoyed by his continued habit of talking to himself. It wasn't just that it was pointless, but that everything he seemed to say was dumb. "Who cares, Taylor, just get back to the ship. Get back and get Sonner. This is our chance!"

The mention and thought of Sonner set him in motion again, back through the walls and bulkheads of the station, back into his own Corvette and even directly through Sonner, causing her to momentarily shiver, before finally returning to the deep space corridor in front of the starlight door. Wasting no time, he ran towards it, back toward consciousness and his chance to rescue Satomi and the others.

THIRTEEN

Taylor opened his silver eyes and sat bolt-upright in the bed that Sonner had re-engineered out of the original stasis table. The bed, like the more clinical table before it, allowed Taylor's simulant body to regenerate, and also his human brain to rest, but it was also what had inadvertently allowed Taylor to tap into the CoreNet and traverse the Fabric.

The door to Taylor's quarters swished open and Sonner came bursting in.

"Don't you knock?" said Taylor, still feeling disorientated as he readjusted to his simulant form from the more ethereal state he had occupied while inside the Fabric.

"The whole station has just gone crazy," Sonner cried, ignoring Taylor's sarcastic comment. Then she saw where he was, still propped up in the bed-come-stasis table. "Did you do this?"

"I think so..." said Taylor, pushing himself out of the bed, still a little groggy. "Either way, we have a window to get on board that other ship without being seen, so we need to move now."

Sonner shot him the sort of look a mom would give a teenage child who'd just rolled in at 3am, without having called. "A little damn warning next time, please!"

"I wanted it to be a surprise..." said Taylor, giving back as much attitude as he was getting. "Come on, with all hell breaking loose, they won't pay any attention to us, and especially not to a Vice Provost."

Sonner looked like she was about to argue back, but then just rolled her eyes. "Fine, but I hope you know what you're doing!"

Taylor considered saying, 'So do I...', but then thought better of it, and instead just rushed after Sonner, who had bolted back down the central corridor of the ship towards the rear cargo bay and access ramp. Taylor caught up with her just as she was sliding a clip into the base of a sidearm from the weapons locker.

"This isn't the O.K. Corral, Commander," said Taylor nodding towards the weapon in Sonner's hand, "we need to do this quietly and not draw attention to ourselves."

"You should have thought about that before sending the base into a state of frenzy," Sonner hit back, holstering the weapon and pulling on her long black coat to help conceal it, "besides, if things do go badly wrong, which they probably will, it's best to be prepared." Sonner closed the weapons locker and hit the release for the ramp.

"Hey, what about me?" said Taylor, looking at the closed locker door.

"I think a simulant with a gun kinda counts as drawing attention to ourselves, don't you?" Sonner replied, her answer thick with condescension.

Taylor considered this, and despite the additional dose of snark from Sonner, reluctantly found himself agreeing. "Fair point."

The ramp hit the deck and the cargo bay was flooded with the sound of chaos. There were screams, panicked cries, electrical sparks, crackling fires, rippling explosions and half a dozen different alarms and sirens all overlapping. It sounded like the end of days.

"Well, this is fun..." said Sonner, now in one hundred percent snark mode, "Come on, Captain Fantastic, this is your plan, so you lead."

Taylor raced out ahead of Sonner, but skidded to a stop a few meters from the bottom of the ramp, shocked by the utter pandemonium unfolding outside, which was even worse than it had sounded from the relative seclusion of the cargo bay. Sonner appeared at his side and shot him another reproving look, but Taylor ignored her and tried to get his bearings. He knew where they needed to go, though getting there would be a lot harder now that he couldn't simply pass through solid walls, and people. "Come on, this way – it's not far..." he said to Sonner, though he had to raise his voice to a near shout, and then rushed out into the throng, brushing panicked Hedalt aside as he cut a path through the crowds, while the ramp to their ship whirred shut behind them.

At first it was heavy going, but as Sonner managed to draw level with Taylor, the sight of a Vice Provost was still enough to make even the most crazed Hedalt steer a wide birth. Soon they had passed through the connecting corridor into the adjacent landing deck.

"How much further?" Sonner shouted, as a thin-faced Hedalt appeared in front of her, saw the uniform and skipped to the side as if avoiding some muck on the ground.

"It's at the far end of the next section," Taylor called back, barging a man out of the way, "the Hunter Corvette is docked in front of the constabulary offices at the far end."

They continued on, but the scene around them was evolving quickly. Confusion and chaos also created opportunity, and while most still fled for cover to avoid being trampled, a number now seemed to be using the distraction to steal and loot, and fighting was breaking out. It was a volatile mix that could ignite at any moment, and they both knew it. Then the fizz of plasma rifles sharped their senses; looters and bandits were one thing, but panic-stricken militia armed with plasma weapons was a far more serious danger. Taylor could see that several militiamen had already lost their cool and were shooting randomly into the crowds, but the two militiamen guarding the hunter Corvette had held their ground at the base of the cargo ramp. Both looked twitchy and on edge – a poor combination of emotions when holding a powerful plasma weapon.

Taylor caught Sonner by the arm, halting her progress as suddenly as if she'd run into a giant spider's web.

"Hey, take it easy, Captain, I prefer my arm attached to my body," Sonner complained, but then Taylor pointed to the armed militiamen guarding the ship and her face fell. "Oh, great."

"Time for Vice Provost Sonner to work her magic," Taylor said, as he let go of her arm and ushered her towards the Hunter Corvette. Sonner glowered at him but took the lead, straightening her back so that she again looked tall and strong, unlike her regular slouchy posture. The guards saw them approach and leveled their rifles at them, before they spotted the uniform and quickly stood down.

"Apologies, Vice Provost," the first said, "I did not realize anyone from Warfare Command was on the Way Station."

"As far as you are concerned, I am not here," said Sonner, slipping back into her Hedalt persona. "Stand aside, I need to get this simulant back on-board." The militiamen hesitated, but Sonner continued walking and, faced with a choice between blocking the path of a senior officer of Warfare Command, or letting her pass, eventually stepped aside.

"Of course, Vice Provost, but the Constable gave orders that none should enter," the militia solider added, nervously.

"The Constable should concern himself with ending this disorder," Sonner snapped without stopping, "and so should you."

"Yes, Vice Provost..." the militiaman answered and then returned his attention to guarding the entrance.

"I think you missed your true vocation," whispered Taylor, "you clearly should have been an actor."

"That was the easy part," said Sonner, "the real trick will be explaining why I'm leaving the ship with more simulants than I came in with..."

Again, Sonner had made a very good point, but

Taylor was determined to stay positive; they had gotten this far on pure guile and he had to believe that Sonner's talent for amateur dramatics would serve them well again in the future.

They passed through the open inner airlock door and into the main central corridor of the Hunter Corvette. Taylor was relieved to discover that the layout looked identical to his own ship, which meant he knew exactly where to go. "Up here, Satomi's quarters were towards the rear!" Taylor called back, setting off at a jog. He reached Satomi's quarters and hit the door release, waiting impatiently for it to slide back into its housing. If he'd still had lungs, he would have been breathless. He darted inside and then stopped dead; in front of him was a simulant body lying on the stasis table, and in the alcove above it was a head – the cranial unit of Casey Valera.

Sonner swung in through the open doorway, spotted Taylor's startled expression, and then noticed the decapitated simulant body and head. "Come on, Captain, snap out of it, we have to move!" she shouted, seemingly unconcerned with the macabre scene.

"She... her... head..." stammered Taylor.

"What did you expect?" said Sonner, pushing ahead of him and then reaching up to grab Casey's cranial unit out of the alcove. "That they would be sitting in their quarters drinking Bourbon and playing poker? Get your brain into gear, Captain; if we're caught on this ship then we're done for!"

Sonner's warning broke Taylor out of his stupor and he rushed forward, grabbing the simulant body of Casey Valera and hauling it over his shoulder like a giant sack of vegetables. Sonner removed her cloak and placed the cranial unit inside the hood, before bundling the rest of the cloak around it and tying it over her shoulder to make an improvised satchel.

"I thought you said these were Satomi's quarters?" Sonner asked, as she finished tightening the knot.

"They should be, or at least they were on my ship," said Taylor, maneuvering himself and Casey's body out of the door. The red sneakers on Casey's feet banged against the door frame, and Taylor apologized, before wincing, hoping that Sonner hadn't heard him. She had.

"I think she's okay, Captain..." said Sonner, raising the snark'o'meter to a whole new level. "Come on!"

A voice echoed along the corridor and they both froze and looked at each other; Sonner reached down and unclipped the fastener on her holster, but she did not yet draw the weapon.

"Remind me again what you were saying about this not being the O.K. Corral..."

FOURTEEN

Taylor chanced a look along the corridor and saw three Hedalt militia approaching; the same two who had been guarding the ship and a third, dressed in a similar uniform, but with gold stripes along the seams.

"Who is in here?!" the one with the gold-striped uniform called out. "This is Constable Dahr, come out at once. This ship is off limits on my orders!"

"Tough choice, Captain; we either fight our way out or talk our way through..." said Sonner.

"Somehow, I think it will end up being both," said Taylor, gloomily. "But let's see how you fare first."

Sonner nodded, stood tall and paced out into the hallway, with Taylor following close behind, walking with a robotic gait and wearing a blank expression.

"What is the meaning of this?!" cried Sonner, surprising the three militiamen with her boldness, "I demand an explanation!"

It was as if Sonner had sucked the very words the constable had intended to speak out of his own mouth and used them against him. He just stammered and faltered, before finally managing to ask. "I... Vice Provost... there was an intruder alert... I came to..."

"Get back outside and end this unrest, at once!" Sonner ordered, not allowing the constable opportunity to recover, all the time advancing towards them, forcing them to backpedal.

Then the constable saw Taylor, with the headless simulant body slung over his shoulder, like a hunter's prize. "But, Vice Provost, this is highly irregular. It is my duty to know!"

Sonner brushed past the constable, "Your duty is to do what I say, now stand aside before I relieve you and have you locked up in your own cells!"

Taylor was again struck by how fiercely impressive Sonner's performance was, and how it compelled the constable to immediately back down. *We're actually going to pull this off!* he thought as Sonner broke through their ranks, but then he saw the constable's reverent expression change; his cheek muscles tightened and his eyes sharpened, as if he'd uncovered a clue in one of his investigations. Taylor followed the line of his gaze and his acute simulant eyes saw what the constable had seen; the make-up on the back of Sonner's neck, no longer concealed by her hooded cloak, which was now carrying Casey's head, had been smudged clean, revealing Sonner's uniquely human skin tone.

"Seize her!" shouted the constable, but Taylor was already moving and the combined weight of him plus another simulant body smashed through the militiamen like a freight train, slamming them against the walls of the corridor and to the deck.

"Run!" shouted Taylor as he raced past Sonner, moving so fast he could scarcely believe it himself; the memories he held of the original Taylor Ray didn't suggest he was much of a sprinter. Sonner set off after him as several volleys of plasma fire flashed past, searing holes into the wall of the corridor. Sonner jinked to the side to throw off their aim, but the next burst hit her thigh, melting the armor plating like candle wax exposed to flame. She cried out as the heat bled through into her flesh and drew her weapon, firing on the move and hitting one of the armed militiamen in the chest. He yelled and fell back, but the constable grabbed the fallen combatant's plasma rifle from his flailing body and continued the pursuit. Taylor's incredible pace had already allowed him to reach the top of ramp leading back down onto the landing deck, and he was again assaulted by the maelstrom of noise from electrical fires, sirens, looting and general mayhem. He checked behind, seeing Sonner close on his tail, and set off down the ramp, but mere steps from the bottom he saw three more armed militiamen rushing towards him. The sound of his heavy boots screeching across the metal ramp drew the attention of the closest militiaman, who raised his weapon and ordered him to halt. With mere milliseconds to think, Taylor's choice shocked even himself; he lifted Casey's headless body off his shoulders and threw it at the militiamen. Plasma shards streaked past both sides of his head as Casey's simulant body piled into the leading soldier like a bowling ball, sending him tumbling out into the throng like a fallen nine-pin. Wasting no time, Taylor ran at the other two, who were too stunned at seeing their comrade bowled over by a headless cadaver to do anything but gawp in astonishment. Taylor swung a fist at the nearest, forgetting his immense strength, and heard bone crunch as the Hedalt militiaman flew backwards like he'd been shot from a catapult. The third soldier fired and Taylor registered an impact on his right shoulder, but felt no pain. Stepping sideways to throw off his assailant's aim he then surged forward, catching the barrel of the rifle and jerking it to the side, flinging the helpless Hedalt mercenary into the air and into the rampaging crowd, where he was trampled underfoot.

Taylor flipped the rifle around and angled it back up the ramp, struggling a little to keep a steady aim as his shoulder seemed to be malfunctioning; the simulant version of an injury, he figured. Sonner was racing down the ramp, still being pursued by the constable and another one of the militiamen, and Taylor fired, hitting the pursuing assailant in the chest with three searing bolts of plasma, killing him instantly. Sonner was still firing blindly at the constable, who shot back, sending a plasma shard glancing across her left side. The armor deflected the energy, but the hit was still enough to unbalance her, and Sonner staggered and fell. But Taylor was already on his way, attention focused solely on the constable like a frenzied bull. The constable's eyes grew wide with terror as he saw Taylor moving at him with freakish speed. He jerked the rifle towards him, but Taylor grabbed the barrel before he could fire and tore it from the constable's grasp, like a mean older sibling stealing a toy from their brother or sister. Remarkably, the constable retained his wits and composure and swung a heavy right cross into Taylor's face, but despite the skill and power behind the blow, it was like punching a block of lead. The constable screamed in agony as his knuckles crunched against Taylor's metal skull, but he didn't have time to nurse the injury, before Taylor landed a more measured cross of his own. Three of the constable's bloodied teeth hit the ramp moments before his unconscious body did.

Taylor rushed over to collect Casey's simulant frame, again slinging it over his shoulders, though this time with more difficultly, since his left arm refused to fully co-operate. "I'm sorry about throwing you..." he said as he adjusted his balance. He knew she couldn't hear him, since her head was still wrapped in Sonner's cloak, looking like a bundle of apples from the market, but after using her body for such an ignominious purpose, he felt an apology was required all the same.

Sonner struggled to her feet and trained the barrel of her sidearm into the crowd, searching for signs of other militiamen, but the throng had thinned and she could only see looters.

Taylor stepped to her side, Casey still slung over his shoulders, "I think we're clear, let's get out of here!" he said, and then he noticed the singed and melted armor plating on Sonner's leg, "Hey, are you okay? Can you make it back to the ship?"

The wounds should have been agony, but for whatever reason Sonner could not feel any pain. All she could think about was that this insane scheme had worked. They should be dead, but instead they had won. They had beaten the odds. And if they alone could beat the Hedalt – a middle-aged engineering officer with an attitude problem and a simulant recreation of a three-hundred-year-old fleet Captain with a sentimental streak as broad as the galactic long bar – imagine what they could do with an entire fleet behind them. Sonner should have felt fear and shock and relief, but she felt none of these emotions. Instead, she felt invincible. She smiled at Taylor and said, "Yes, I can make it back. Lead the way, Captain Taylor Ray!"

FIFTEEN

Taylor and Sonner made it safely back to the Contingency One without further incident. No-one looked at them closely, despite the fact that Taylor was hauling a decapitated body over his shoulders. This was because the majority of Hedalt who were still running around in the half-lit chaos were looters, who were also carrying something over their shoulders or bundled up into bags or makeshift satchels, like Sonner.

At Sonner's instruction, Taylor had placed Casey's body on the table in the ship's workshop. He was now monitoring the on-going status of the space station through a computer console to the side, while Sonner unbundled Casey's head and worked on re-attaching it to the body.

"It looks like things are getting back to normal

outside," commented Taylor. "They've shut off the alarms and restored power to most sections. It looks like the militia are gaining an upper hand on the looters too."

"Let's just hope your little trick also knocked out the security camera feeds, otherwise we may have a visit from our constable friend," Sonner replied, as she manipulated Casey's head into position. Then she let out a sudden, sharp breath as she shifted weight onto her injured leg. Taylor had forgotten that Sonner had been hit during their escape; he grabbed an emergency medical kit from the wall – another recent addition as part of Sonner's on-going modifications to the ship – and slapped it down on the workbench next to Casey's head.

Sonner looked at it and then scowled at Taylor, "I'm fine, don't fuss."

"You were shot with a plasma rifle," Taylor said, correcting her. "That replica Hedalt armor may have absorbed the brunt of it, but you're still hurt, so swallow that stubborn pride and let me help you."

"Fine, just make it quick," said Sonner as she returned to her work, still scowling.

Taylor opened the medical kit, removed the tools that he needed and then knelt down to inspect Sonner's injured thigh. "Besides, I'm going to need you to return the favor," he added, while pulling away the remains of the melted armor plating, exposing her upper thigh and drawing piercing looks from Sonner. "My shoulder took a hit and isn't functioning properly." He tore back the dense fabric around the wound and reached up to grab the stem-cell regenerator.

"Hey, do you mind?" Sonner said to the top of Taylor's head. Her tone was icy and she tried to wrestle her leg away from Taylor's ministrations. "The last man who got that close to my thighs was my ex-husband."

"Well, it's a good job that I'm an android and not a man then, isn't it?" said Taylor, already growing fed up with his difficult patient. "Stop fidgeting already!" he snapped, "this won't take a minute."

Sonner scowled again and finally stood still. "That's what my ex-husband used to say. Fine, get on with it."

Taylor used the stem-cell regenerator to repair the burn damage and then swapped the tool for a bandage spray, covering the area with a thin blue gel that instantly dried, giving Sonner's skin the plasticine appearance of Taylor's. "There, all done," he said, standing up and packing the tools back into the medical kit. "Now you look like me, except bluer."

Sonner peered down at the exposed area of her thigh, observing how the new blue patch seemed to flex and flow with her movements. "Not bad, thanks." Then she nodded towards Taylor's damaged shoulder. "I'll sort you out when you're unconscious in bed."

"What the hell?" said Taylor.

"That didn't quite come out quite right," admitted Sonner.

"I'm beginning to understand why you're no longer married," Taylor quipped, smirking.

Sonner's laser-like glare soon wiped the smirk of Taylor's face. "What I mean is while you're in the DMZ, interfacing with your friend here."

Taylor frowned, "The what?"

"Right, I haven't told you about my little invention here, have I?"

"I saw you working on it before I sent the station into meltdown, but no, you haven't," said Taylor.

"From the scans I took of your own cranial unit..."

Taylor faked a cough.

"Sorry, I mean your dainty little head," Sonner corrected herself. "Anyway, I was able to identify several unique differences between your head and scans of simulants captured during the war, which are stored in the fleet archives I transferred over from the base, and also this young lady here."

"What differences?" asked Taylor, leaning in to get a closer look at Casey, whose head was now fully re-attached. She looked exactly the same as the Casey he remembered seeing back on the Contingency base; the Casey that Sonner had shot and killed, before he and the Commander had declared amnesty. Perhaps it was fitting that Sonner would give life back to another version of Casey. Even if it wasn't the same person he'd known, it was close enough – a second chance that most people don't get.

"Your brain may be organic, but there are a number of neural interfaces that feed your conscious mind into the CoreNet and allow the Hedalt to manipulate your experiences," said Sonner, while continuing to enter a rapid sequence of commands into the console. "In your head, some of these connections overloaded and were severed, but also some interfaces that are buried deeper inside your brain seemed to reconnect. Certainly, the Casey Valera here shows no sign of such a connection in her brain."

Taylor frowned, "So, what do these 'deeper connections' actually do?"

Sonner sniffed and half-shrugged, "Just a guess, but I'd say it perhaps could explain your newfound magical powers inside the Fabric." Then she pointed to a scan of Casey's head on the console screen in front of her and indicated to several sections just underneath her metal skull. "These neural interfaces I do understand, though," she went one. "These appear to be what allowed the

Hedalt to manipulate you and exert control over your cognitive state. My guess is that by some freak of chance, your fall managed to pop these circuits while rebooting the deep transceiver interfaces that let you dial-in to the CoreNet."

"Maybe it wasn't chance," said Taylor, giving a little shrug, "maybe it was fate."

"And maybe Elvis is still alive and cruising around the Orion Nebula in a flying saucer," Sonner said, looking down her nose at him.

"Anything is possible..."

Sonner rolled her eyes and continued with her analysis. "As I was saying, your friend here obviously still has all of these surface-level neural interfaces intact. But now I know which ones to sever, I can, for want of a better phrase, 'wake her up'."

Taylor could sense there was a 'but' coming, and he wasn't wrong.

"But," Sonner went on, as if on cue, "the technology that allows you to jaunt around inside the Fabric is way too complex for my puny human brain to understand. And it's buried too deep in the brain tissue too. Messing with it is a risk I'd rather not take."

"So, does that mean she'll be different to me, somehow?" said Taylor, suddenly concerned that Casey wouldn't experience the same freedom of thought as he did.

"I certainly hope so," quipped Sonner, "because one of you is bad enough." Taylor now rolled his eyes. "But no, she'll be conscious of what she is, exactly the same as you are, but she won't be able to enter the Fabric and influence the CoreNet. That skill is unique to one Taylor Ray."

Taylor nodded. It would have been helpful if Casey shared his peculiar talent, but life and freedom from the Hedalt's deception was more important. "I can live with that, and I'm sure she can too," he answered. Excitement was building in his mind now, but then he remembered how much of a struggle it had been for him to come to terms with what he was. "I don't know how she'll react to discovering what she is. She's young, and a dreamer; maybe reality is worse than the fiction she's living now."

"Worse than being a slave to an empire that tried to wipe out the human race?"

"You know what I mean," snapped Taylor. "Sometimes, ignorance is bliss."

Sonner gave Taylor what could only be described as a dirty look, "I know you don't believe that, Captain. You're a realist. You deal in facts, not fantasy."

"I used to believe that," Taylor admitted, "but things are different now. I can accept what I am; I just don't know if she can."

"Only one way to find out, Captain," said

Sonner, brightly. "Don't make the choice for her; she's likely stronger than you think. Besides, I think I have a way to perhaps give her an advantage that you didn't have." Sonner tapped the table that Casey was lying on, "With this interface I can create a DMZ, or demilitarized zone, where you and Casey can meet, before I wake her up."

"What's this DMZ do?"

"It's basically a safe space for your minds," Sonner went on, enthusiasm building in her tone and mannerisms, as it always did when she began talking about some clever piece of tech or engineering. "It's like the CoreNet, but detached from it. A bit like how you described the deep space corridor, before you passed through the starlight door, except that you can both exist there." Then she smiled, "Sort of a virtual chat room. Or perhaps more of a prep room."

"Preparation for what?"

"For real life, Captain," said Sonner. "You'll have a chance to tell Casey what she is, before she has to face it for real."

"But what if she doesn't want to face it? What if she says no?"

Sonner chewed the inside of her mouth; clearly, that possibility had not occurred to her. "I'm afraid if we do this then she won't have a choice. I can't create the DMZ while she's still hooked into the

Hedalt neural interfaces. I have to cut the cord first, and after I do, there's no going back."

Taylor closed his eyes and let his chin drop to his chest. The question of whether Casey, or indeed any of his other crew mates, would actually want to be woken up hadn't even crossed his mind, until he'd posed the question to Sonner. He tried to ask himself what he would have chosen, if he'd been given a choice, but it was an impossible question to answer. Faced with the ugly truth – that you would be forced to live inside a synthetic frame that could no longer physically experience emotions – he might have said no. But it was also true that he had adapted to his new form remarkably smoothly, so much so that it now felt completely natural to him. Perhaps this was because he'd never truly been human, but whatever the reason, his experiences had shown him that it was possible to adapt, and be comfortable in this new skin. If he could do it then so could Casey.

"Decision time, Captain, are we doing this or not?" said Sonner, as the silence became awkward.

Taylor opened his eyes and peered down at the simulant form of Casey Valera, torn between the choice of offering her a new life – a real life – or allowing her to continue the Hedalt fiction, where she soared through the stars with her sequined sneakers resting on top of the pilot's console. Then he suddenly remembered the mint that he'd found tucked down the side of the pilot's chair and he pulled it out of his pocket. It was a symbol of the fantasy the Hedalt had created for her, to keep her compliant and manipulate her into hunting out any humans who managed to flee and survive, or that still remained hidden, as Sonner had been. Taylor shook his head. *No...* he thought, *she wouldn't want to be used like that. She wouldn't want to live a lie.* He placed the mint into Casey's jacket pocket and then looked up at Sonner. "Yes, we're doing this."

SIXTEEN

Taylor stood waiting in the DMZ, which appeared as a recreation of the Corvette's cargo bay, except that instead of the rear ramp lowering onto a landing deck, it extended out into deep space. It was a stunning view, if also a little disconcerting. Sonner had explained that it would be better to get Taylor set up in the DMZ first, so that he would be the first thing that Casey saw when she eventually appeared, if indeed Sonner was successful in severing the neural interfaces that governed the Hedalt control systems.

He had been inside the DMZ for perhaps ten minutes – it was difficult to judge the passage of time so it could have been shorter or longer – but it had been more than enough time for Taylor to realize he had no idea what he would say when

Casey appeared. He chastised himself for not having considered this sooner, but the opportunity to rescue a member of his crew had presented itself more suddenly than he'd expected, and he had simply been swept up in events and caught unprepared.

In her innately blunt and unsympathetic manner, Sonner's advice was to simply tell her the truth, arrow straight. It was a method that may have worked with Blake, but he imagined that Casey would need a more nuanced approach. Not that it mattered, because he didn't have much of a choice. There was no sugar-coating what she was, or what she was about to face, and the harsh reality was that once Sonner had severed the neural connections, she had no option but to face it. He hoped that she would be able to live with what she'd become. He hoped she would forgive him.

"Captain?"

Taylor spun around to see Casey a few meters away. She was dressed in her uniform, the same as Taylor, except she always left the top two buttons of her shirt undone, revealing a red vest top underneath. On her feet she wore red sneakers in place of the regulation issue boots. These appeared to be the same red sneakers that her physical counterpart had been wearing, and were classic Casey – colorful protests against the strict Earth Fleet uniform code. Taylor had never bothered to enforce the code, since they had been thousands of light years from the nearest Earth Fleet outpost, and if he was being honest, he liked that Casey brightened up the often sterile interior of their ship. Or at least that was his memory; how much was real and how much was a fiction the Hedalt had invented, he'd never know.

"Casey, hi..." said Taylor, managing to open with an even dumber line than he had expected.

"What are we doing in the cargo bay?" said Casey, sounding anxious, but not afraid. If anything, she sounded irritated. Then she peered outside through the lowered cargo ramp, "Are we in space? How can the ramp be down if we're in space?"

"This is going to take some explaining, Casey, and I won't lie to you, what I'm going to tell you will be hard to hear," Taylor said, finally getting into gear, "but I promise you it's the truth."

"Dang, I knew I shouldn't have eaten that cheese roll before bed," said Casey, stepping onto the ramp and peering out into space. "I thought it smelled a little off, but wow, this is the craziest cheese dream I've ever had."

"Casey, this isn't a dream. I wish it was." Taylor could see that she was trying to mask her unease with humor, and watched as Casey folded her arms across her chest, muscles tensing up, as if a sharp sea breeze had suddenly whisked over her.

"So if it's not a dream then what is this?" she said, her words spiked with more aggression than Taylor was used to hearing from her. "We were on the ship and..." then she hesitated and scowled, "what were we doing? I can't remember." Then she unfolded her arms and took a step closer to Taylor, her eyes imploring him for answers. "I feel... different, Captain. It's like I've forgotten something, or lost something. I can't explain it."

Taylor closed the distance between them and gently held Casey's shoulders. "Look, there's no easy way to say it, so I'll just say it. All I ask is that you hear me out, and don't just dismiss what I'm telling you, no matter how crazy it sounds."

"Crazier than talking to my Captain in the cargo bay with the door wide open into deep space?" said Casey, managing a weak smile.

"Casey, you're not who you think you are, and I'm not the Taylor Ray you think I am either," said Taylor and he could feel Casey's shoulder's hunch a little. "What you remember is a lie, created by the Hedalt as a means of control. Earth lost the war, over three hundred years ago."

Casey backed away from Taylor, but did not speak. She just looked at him as if he'd just admitted to being a serial killer.

"I know it sounds crazy, but hear me out," Taylor continued. "The Hedalt Empire nuked Earth and wiped out humanity, or close enough, and those that survived scattered and ran. The Hedalt then used the engineered human brains of former Earth Fleet officers to crew what they called Hunter Corvettes, ships designed to chase down and kill the survivors. You remember how the Hedalt can't handle space travel? They needed a crew that could. That was us, Casey – me, you, Blake and Satomi. They made us, put our brains into synthetic bodies, and used neural interfaces to manipulate what we saw and thought and did."

"Captain, stop this, it's not funny!" Casey shouted, now looking terrified. She ran to the door of the cargo hold and pulled on the handle, but it would not open. She hammered her fists on it, but the pounding generated no sound. "I want to get out of here. I want to wake up. Let me out!"

"Casey, I can let you out. I will let you out."

"Then do it!"

"When I do, you'll wake up in the workshop on the ship, and you'll see that I'm telling you the truth," said Taylor, trying to remain calm and rational. "You'll see me, but I won't look like the Taylor you remember. And you won't look or feel the same either; not the same as you feel in here."

Casey pushed off from the door and pressed her back against it, "It's just a dream, Casey, it's just a dream. Stay calm and you'll just wake up. Stay calm... Stay calm..."

Taylor knew he had to reach her somehow, but

he couldn't blame her for reacting as she had done; everything he'd told her sounded insane, and in retrospect their frankly unbelievable deep-space location probably hadn't helped either. He tried to think of another approach, another way to tell her the truth in a way that didn't seem like the ravings of a lunatic. *Damn it, Casey, I wish you could hear me!* he screamed inside his head, willing his human brain to come up with a human solution to an alien problem.

Casey's eyes grew wide, "What did you say?"

Taylor frowned. *Did you just hear that?*

"Yes, damn it, I can hear you, but your lips aren't moving!" said Casey.

The DMZ... Taylor realized. The DMZ was built on the same technology as the CoreNet, and so inside this place they existed as pure thought. And if Casey was in this place with him then perhaps they could exist in each other's thoughts too. He didn't have to use words to explain what was happening to Casey; all he had to do was let her see inside his mind and experience what he had experienced, like a computer download. He took himself back to the memory of the mission that had led them to the moon and the Contingency base, and then closed his eyes. He could feel Casey in there with him, and then she appeared, looking calmer and more at ease.

"What is this?" said Casey. "I don't remember

this mission." They were both on the bridge of the Corvette, watching themselves as if watching a perfect holographic reproduction of a memory. Casey moved over to the pilot's console and stared at her doppelganger, and her purple sparkling footwear. "I don't have sneakers like that. And I'm wearing my hair differently. Is this the future?"

"It's actually the past", said Taylor, "but it's not a part of your past. This is a different Casey Valera. Another simulant recreation of you. This Casey Valera was a member of my crew."

"I don't understand," said Casey. She was no longer afraid. The act of entering each other's minds seemed to have completely changed the dynamic between them, as if the human instinct to fear the unknown and the corresponding fight or flight response to threats had been switched off.

"Then let me show you..."

Time accelerated, but so did their thoughts and perceptions, as Taylor took them both through the events that led up to the moment where Taylor had been confronted by Commander Sarah Sonner on the Contingency base. She saw what Taylor had seen and felt what he had felt. She saw Blake fall and the other Casey lift the girder off him in an impossible feat of strength, and then he saw Taylor go after what he'd believed to be a Hedalt solider alone, only to fall from the tower of containers and slam his head into the deck. And then she saw the deep space corridor, and the memories of the real Taylor Ray's home on Earth by the Columbia River, where she had drunk whiskey with him on the balcony. And then she saw Satomi and her own counterpart being shot, and Taylor waking again, bound to a chair, and being given the cold, hard truth by a human female officer. The scene moved on, fast and relentless, but no detail was spared until they reached the Hedalt Way Station. Casey saw the female officer and the simulant version of Taylor breaking into the Hunter Corvette, and then escaping with her synthetic body over Taylor's shoulders and her head bundled into the woman's coat. And then their minds separated, and they were back in the cargo bay, both on their knees and holding each other's hands, heads spinning as if they'd drunk too much.

"I don't believe it..." said Casey, barely louder than a whisper. But despite her words, Taylor knew she had accepted what she'd seen.

"I struggle to believe it too, Casey," said Taylor, "but it is what we are. It's the truth."

"But why did you come for me? Your Casey Valera is dead. I'm not the person you knew."

Taylor got to his feet and helped Casey to stand. Their hands remained clasped together and he could feel her body shaking. "Yes, it's true you're a different Casey. Your experiences are different..."

he pointed down at her bright red sneakers, "and your taste in footwear is different," then he added, smiling, "though not by much," and Casey smiled back. "But in every other way, you're the same Casey Valera I knew, and I'm the same Taylor Ray. Except that we're no longer puppets on a string, Casey. We're real. We're free. And we have a chance to hit back at the bastards that did this to us."

Casey let go of Taylor's hands and peered out of the open bay door. She shook her head and let out a long, low whistle. "So what happens now?"

Taylor stood by her side. "Now we wake up."

SEVENTEEN

Casey Valera sat on the workbench in the workshop with her head in her hands, palms pressed tightly over her new silver simulant eyes. She had been this way for several minutes, after waking up to the reality of what she was. The first person she had seen was Commander Sarah Sonner, who had backed away to the side of the workshop to give the newly awakened simulant some space, though she still watched her keenly, trying to predict her actions. Casey did not yet know of her super-human strength, though Sonner was deeply wary of her abilities and did not want to appear a threat, especially since she had been responsible for killing another version of her. Taylor had entered soon after, using his own simulant legs to sprint from his quarters with

155

inhuman speed, and it had been his sudden and shock appearance that had set Casey into a spiral of denial.

"This can't be real... it just can't be..." Casey was saying to herself, over and over again. Taylor had tried to comfort her, tried to empathize as only he could, but despite the connection they had made inside the DMZ and inside each other's minds, the real-world reality of Casey's new life was simply overwhelming.

"You're just going to have to give her time," said Sonner, as she tentatively stepped to Taylor's side. Both had their backs pressed to the wall of the workshop. Unusually for Sonner, her tone and manner were comforting and encouraging, rather than prickly and impatient. "She'll come around. She'll have to."

"I know..." said Taylor, though it was half-hearted. What Sonner had said was logical, but it was not true that accepting her new reality was the only option for her. Taylor had managed to accept what he was, perhaps because his desire to rescue and wake his crew members was more powerful than the hopelessness that had threatened to consume him. Casey had not yet discovered her purpose, and he recognized the well of despair that was opening up beneath her. Casey had always been the brightest and most optimistic person he had ever known. It didn't matter if his memories of her were the real Taylor's or even if they were manufactured by the Hedalt – the Casey Valera he knew loved to live. But this was not the Casey Valera that he had known. This was a unique Casey Valera, born for the first time, and so he could not begin to fathom what was going on inside her head.

"We should get off this station as soon as possible," Sonner added, conscious that they had spent too long in one place already, and especially in light of the recent excitement. Ship docking and departures had not been suspended, but once the constabulary had fully regained order and discovered the theft of a simulant – the property of Warfare Command – it was entirely possible, and even likely, they would ground all ships and begin a search. "I've already requested a departure slot, and thanks to our friend Sub-Deck Chief Mallor, we'll get bumped to the head of the queue."

Taylor nodded. He didn't want to divert his attention from Casey at the point where she was most vulnerable and disorientated, but Sonner was right; they couldn't risk being trapped on the Way Station. "Is our black market transceiver installed and ready?"

"Yes, and it's working perfectly," said Sonner, with more than a hint of pride, "That device is like a skeleton key; it will allow us to pass through this Way Station and any other outpost or waypoint we might encounter en-route."

Taylor sighed; it was an involuntary, human reaction, and it made Sonner smile. "It still amazes me that you do things like that."

"What? Agree with you?" Taylor answered with a wry smile.

"Very funny, Captain. I'll start the departure process from here, but you should get to the bridge. It looks like you're still our pilot, for the time being at least."

"Aye aye, Commander Sarah Sonner," said Taylor slightly wearily.

"Hey, don't worry Captain," said Sonner, suddenly becoming more heartfelt again. She placed a hand onto Taylor's newly-repaired shoulder and gave the fabric of his jacket a gentle tug, "Look how far you've come, in such a short space of time. She'll make it too, I know she will."

Taylor returned the warm smile and nodded, before leaving the workshop and heading to the bridge. Sonner paused only to input the departure request into the computer console and then shot a last fleeting look at Casey, considering whether to explain to her what they were doing, but figured that she likely wouldn't be able to process it along with everything else rushing through her fragile human brain, and so she left without another word.

Unknown to the others, Casey's enhanced simulant hearing had picked up Taylor's earlier response to Sonner, and had recognized it instantly as an adaptation of her own catch-phrase when responding to orders. Hearing Taylor speak it was like hearing him speak a magic word, except rather than casting a spell, it had broken the one that Casey had been under since her awakening. Spreading her fingers just enough to peer through, she had watched the interaction between Sonner and Taylor. Her enhanced eyes picked up their subtle changes in facial expression and body language, and despite their obvious physical differences, Casey could see that there was a connection between them; a connection that was unmistakably, deeply human.

When the door to the workshop slid shut, leaving her alone, she dropped her hands and rested them on her thighs, looking at them as if they were exhibits in a Victorian freak show. Then she looked down and saw the bright red sneakers on her feet and laughed, surprising herself that she was able to reproduce the sound. It seemed absurd that the sneakers were the genuine article, but the feet that wore them were artificial. She tried wiggling her toes; they felt real enough.

"Casey Valera, what are you going to do?" she said out loud, before sliding her hands into the pockets of her uniform jacket. Her fingers touched a small object and she removed it, holding it out in front of her face, before laughing again, this time far more freely and deeply, and without any concern for the strangeness of her own voice. The object in her hand was the mint that Taylor had found hidden down the side of the pilot's chair, and had slipped into Casey's pocket while she was still unconscious.

She closed her hand around the candy and smiled.

EIGHTEEN

The unoccupied mission ops console suddenly started to bleep angrily as the ship was regurgitated back up through the belly of the decrepit Hedalt Way Station and into the outer launch bay, ready for departure. Taylor frowned, wondering what the cause of the urgent alarm was, and peered over his shoulder from his position in the pilot's chair to catch Sonner with a similarly baffled expression.

"Are you going to get that?" asked Taylor, impatiently, as the sound of the alarm continued to saturate the bridge. It was beginning to get on his nerves, or the simulant equivalent of them, "someone has to steer this thing..."

Sonner pushed herself out of the command chair, grumbling, "We need a bigger crew."

"Well, if this new transceiver actually works and we can jump, you might just get your wish."

Sonner didn't answer and just trudged over to the mission ops console, begrudging the need to get up from her comfortable seat. Just as she reached it the docking lift reached its apex and locked into position. Taylor could see from his instruments that the outer dock had already begun to depressurize, ready for them to depart.

"Damn it," cursed Sonner, "We have a problem."

Taylor spun the pilot's chair around to face her; if he'd had a gut, there would have been a sinking feeling inside it. "What's up?"

"They've just put all departures on hold, station-wide," said Sonner, frantically tapping commands into the console. "I'm trying to bluff our way out using my 'Vice Provost' act, but they're not buying it."

Taylor's scowl deepened and he was about to suggest Sonner make the demand more forcefully when another alert sounded, this time from the tactical console. If there was one station on the bridge where an alert meant bad news, it was the tactical station, and from the sudden look of concern on Sonner's face, she realized it too. Taylor sprang out of the pilot's chair, making it to the tactical station before Sonner, who was no longer trudging around the bridge, but practically sprinting.

"What is it?" Sonner asked. The breath from her voice almost turned to frost.

"A ship just jumped in," replied Taylor with matching soberness. "I don't know what it is, but it's big. Wait, there's an unencoded transmission coming through from it, text only."

Taylor punched a few commands and brought up the message on the console screen. The message read, 'All ships are ordered to remain grounded and submit for inspection, by order of Provost Adra of Warfare Command. Any ship attempting to leave the Way Station without authorization will be destroyed. Message ends.'

"We need to get out of here, quickly," said Sonner, wasting no time. "Start the jump calculations now, we'll have to part-compute the course before synchronizing with the super-luminal transceiver out there."

Taylor nodded and rushed back to the pilot's console, "Even if we start now, we can't complete the final computations without synchronizing with the CoreNet; it's the only way to jump along the threads."

"I know that, Captain, but we have no choice," said Sonner, frostily, "You'll just have to keep us out of range of that ship, until we can jump."

"Damn it, I knew you were going to say that," said Taylor as he initiated the jump program and began to warm up the jump engines. "Can we just jump from inside the station?"

"Not unless you want your atoms spread out across the cosmos," Sonner answered, sliding into the chair in front of the tactical console. Taylor heard the low thrum of the weapons systems coming online. "You're just going to have to fly fast and loose and hope their aim is a bad as their manners."

"I'm not flying anywhere with the launch bay doors closed," said Taylor, pointing to the image on the viewport of the giant slab of metal that was currently barring their exit.

"Let me worry about that. You just be ready to fly once we break out of here."

"Break out?" Taylor replied, glancing over to Sonner. "You're not seriously going to blow open the launch bay?" Sonner didn't answer, but from the look on her face, Taylor knew she was deadly serious. "I thought you were set against spreading our atoms into space?"

"No guts, no glory, Captain!" said Sonner, enthusiastically, "Besides, unless you have another suggestion, I don't see that we have a choice."

Taylor pulled the manual control column closer and got ready to maneuver the ship. "My guts are made of some unknown metals and polymers, and I've no interest in glory."

"Fine, then I'll just rely on your human instinct

to want to stay alive," said Sonner. "Are you ready?"

"No, but like you said, what choice do we have?"

Sonner took a deep breath and locked the forward cannons onto the central mass of the launch bay doors. "Firing in three... two... one..." The ship lurched back as the forward cannons erupted, butting up against the rear bulkhead of the outer launch bay, and then as the bay doors were blasted open the remaining pressure in the bay blew them forwards. Taylor could hear and feel the scraping of the hull against the deck of the launch bay and wrestled with the control column to steady their course, before pushing the thrusters hard forwards. Seconds later they smashed through the mangled remains of the bay doors, as if the station had abruptly belched them out into space. More alarms sounded on the bridge and Taylor saw the damage alerts pop up in his secondary console, though he had no idea how bad it was.

"We're still flying, so don't worry about the alarms," Sonner shouted over to him from the tactical console, as if she'd read his mind. "Just keep us away from that big ship."

Taylor throttled up the main engines and locked in the relative position of Provost Adra's ship into the computer. He then threw up an image of the ship into a window on the main viewport, before steering in the opposite direction. He stole a look at their potential new adversary on the viewport and wished he hadn't. He instantly recognized the ship's design as being the same as the one he'd seen while in the Fabric. Set against the backdrop of space it had been impossible to accurately judge its size, but with the Way Station for scale the colossal proportions of this machine of war were plain to see, and he realized the odds of them escaping its reach had just plummeted.

Sonner whistled, "They didn't have those three-hundred years ago. That thing has got to be three times our size."

"It's closer to four," Taylor corrected her as the scans of the Hedalt warship appeared on his console. Interfacing with the docking computer on the Way Station had uploaded some new data to their systems, and the vessel read as a Hedalt War Frigate. "Hold on, it's coming straight for us..." Taylor called out as the bigger ship powered towards them.

Taylor pushed the engines of the Corvette as hard as he could without taking them beyond the sync range of the super-luminal transceiver. If he flew out of range, they would lose synchronization and have to restart the jump sequence all over again, and that was time they didn't have to spare.

"Swing the ship back around to face it," Sonner called out, "Maybe if I can pop them on the nose with the forward cannons, they might think twice about coming on so strong."

Taylor complied, pulsing the thrusters to point the fore of the Contingency One at the oncoming frigate and then saw the cannon fire erupt through the main viewport and streak towards the enemy ship, hitting it on the mid-dorsal section. "Got it!" cried Sonner, but then her face fell, "Minimal damage. Damn that thing is tough..."

"They're firing back!" Taylor shouted, jerking the controls to the right in a desperate attempt to fight their momentum and change course; streaks of the plasma flashed past the viewport and then they were hit. Taylor was thrown to the deck as the lights on the bridge flickered wildly and the mission ops console burst into sparks of blue flame. He pushed himself up and flung himself back into his chair, grabbing the controls and fighting again to change their course. He glanced over to see Sonner slumped forward on the tactical console, blood trickling from her forehead where it had collided with the instruments.

"Commander, are you okay?" he called out, trying to rally her, but there was no answer, "Commander Sonner!" he called out, but again no answer. The controls were still responding and Taylor was able to reduce the ship's speed, keeping it on thrusters to remain more maneuverable, but this had allowed the frigate to close the distance between them. A voice transmission from the enemy vessel blared out through the speakers on the bridge. "Unregistered Corvette, power down your weapons and engines and prepare to be boarded. Fail to comply and you will be destroyed."

"Like hell!" Taylor shouted, slamming the controls forward in an attempt to get behind the frigate and find a blind spot, but again flashes of plasma dashed by and he felt their Corvette take another hit. More alarms sounded, but the damage was not critical. Nevertheless, Taylor knew they couldn't take many more hits like that; even one more could cripple them. He again glanced across to Sonner, but she was still out cold, and then he checked his navigation console to view the progress of the jump calculations. *Damn it, too slow... too slow!*

"What the hell is going on?"

Taylor jerked around to see Casey Valera standing just inside the bridge; with all the commotion, he hadn't heard the door swoosh open.

"We're under attack!" Taylor shouted back, before concentrating into the pilot's viewport to avoid another barrage of incoming fire..

"I can see that, Captain..." Casey answered as she rushed closer, stumbling and catching herself on the command chair as another plasma shard glanced across their aft quarter. The metal frame of the chair creaked and gave way under the pressure of her grip. Casey released the crumpled metal on the chair and looked at her hand in amazement.

"You get used to it," said Taylor. "Can you check on Sonner, she looks hurt?"

Casey darted forward and appeared beside Taylor, peering down at him with an expectant look. Taylor frowned back at her briefly, before more flashes on the viewport forced him to make another desperate evasive maneuver, avoiding the plasma shards by the narrowest of margins, and mostly as a result of luck, rather than piloting skill.

"Are you going to get out of my chair or not, Cap?" said Casey, deciding she had to spell it out for him, but her words seemed to have the opposite effect on Taylor, freezing him to the chair as if he'd been dipped in liquid nitrogen. "You're still sitting there..." Casey added, surprisingly coolly, and this time Taylor did move, springing out of the seat like a jack-in-the-box.

Taylor felt like hugging her, but instead he rushed over to the command chair and sank into it, "Keep that hulk out there from destroying us for another minute, and we'll be able to jump."

"Aye aye, Captain Taylor Ray..." Casey called back, taking up the controls and flipping an army of switches and controls with a speed and precision that Taylor knew only Casey could manage. And then the little Corvette soared, as if it were a phoenix freshly reborn from the ashes and given new life and purpose. Taylor wanted to scream; if he'd had a heart, it would have burst with joy. He checked the jump status on the command chair, willing the computer to work faster, but now there seemed less urgency, as Casey was not only evading the frigate's increasingly frenzied attempts to destroy them, but she was literally flying rings around it.

"Thirty seconds!" shouted Taylor, while glancing again at Sonner, who seemed to be stirring slightly. *Hang on in there, Commander!* He couldn't have the sole human being left in the galaxy dying on his watch, but with Casey at the helm he now no longer felt afraid. The odds had suddenly flipped in their favor.

The whine of the jump engines began to build, as Casey effortlessly skimmed under the belly of the War Frigate and burned the main engines, putting them directly on course for the super-luminal transceiver. The stresses and strains on the hull grew and more alerts sounded, but no sooner had Casey begun the maneuver, she reversed it, pulling the Corvette to a stop right on the jump line, with the frigate floundering in the distance, unable to get a clean shot.

Casey threw up her hands and spun around and

around in her chair, red sneakers flashing like a warning beacon; a beacon that signaled to Hedalt Warfare Command that Earth wasn't done fighting yet. Not by a long shot. Casey Valera's simulant voice filled the bridge, drowning out the alarms and crackling electrical fires and filling Taylor with hope.

"Jumping in five...

...F o u r

...T h r e e

... T   w   o

. . . O   n   e ...

NINETEEN

Constable Dhar massaged his aching jaw and gums –after-effects of the punch he'd taken from the simulant who had raided the Corvette – while he waited anxiously at the airlock door. The umbilical tunnel that connected the Way Station to the newly-arrived Hedalt War Frigate had just finished pressurizing, which meant his new visitors would soon arrive. The frigate was far too big to be docked inside the station, but even the sight of one of Warfare Command's most powerful vessels hanging ominously outside the viewing gallery windows was enough to strike terror into Dhar's heart.

The Way Station would sometimes receive smaller ships from Warfare Command, such as the Hunter Corvette that had docked for refueling, but a ship of this size and class was rare. Their barely-functional installation at the edge of the empire was far too remote to merit any attention from the upper echelons of Warfare Command's hierarchy. But now there was a full Provost waiting on the other side of the airlock door, waiting to question him as to how a ship had escaped, despite her order to lock down the dock, and how a high-functioning simulant that was supposed to be under his guard had been stolen.

Dhar's foot tapped against the deck plating in short staccato bursts, as if he was signaling in Morse code, but as the airlock door finally hissed open his foot froze, along with the rest of his body. At the other end of the long corridor he could see two Hedalt officers pacing towards them, and with each heavy clump of their boots his heart thumped harder and faster.

Dhar's deputy, a young Hedalt female called Nima, stood a few paces behind. With the recent commotion and sudden arrival of the frigate, Dhar hadn't had a chance to speak to Nima about protocol when dealing with their visitors, and was suddenly panicked over what she might say, if pressed. He turned to her, face pale and taut with stress.

"You are not to speak unless asked a direct question, do you understand?" Dhar said. He kept his voice deliberately low, yet despite the reduced volume it conveyed no less malice.

"Yes, Constable," said Nima, flatly.

Dhar was both impressed and irritated that she appeared to be maintaining her composure better than he was. But then she wasn't responsible for allowing a ship to escape and losing a rare and valuable simulant.

"And if you *are* asked a question, keep your answers short and don't volunteer anything you don't have to," Dhar added. "And whatever you do, don't question them. Ever. Even if what they're asking makes no sense to you, just answer as quickly as possible and then hold your tongue."

"But I should tell them the truth?" Nima asked, unsure as to whether Dhar was asking her to be deliberately evasive or merely succinct.

"What truth?" Dhar spat, wishing now that he hadn't brought Nima with him, even though protocol dictated his deputy should accompany him to greet such a high-ranking officer. "That we let an impostor posing as a Vice Provost start a riot and then steal one of their precious Hunter simulants? How do you think that will play out for us?"

Nima felt like reminding Dhar that it was he who had allowed the unknown thieves to make off with the simulant, but despite what Dhar thought, she was smarter than he gave her credit for. She understood the gist of what he was saying, which was in essence, 'don't say anything that's likely to get you posted to a worse dump than this one, or even killed.' That didn't preclude her from dropping Dhar in the dirt, should it become necessary, however. And if it meant saving her own skin she wouldn't hesitate to do so, knowing that Dhar was likely already trying to figure out a way to blame the whole mess on her. As it turned out, there was no opportunity to respond, as the thud of the two Hedalt officer's boots had grown loud enough to focus Dhar's attention back ahead.

Provost Adra stepped from the umbilical and onto the docking platform, wearing a long coat over her armored uniform. Lux flanked her, dressed in a similar uniform, though with less ornate embellishments as befitting his more junior rank, yet Lux still far outranked everyone on the Way Station. Adra looked at Dhar briefly then glanced at Nima and quickly surveyed the surroundings. The whole station was dank and decaying and everything about it, down to the musky odor, repulsed Adra. She detested places like this; the outposts and moons and Way Stations where those who were too feeble-minded to capitalize on their rare gift of being able to withstand super-luminal travel congregated and festered. Way Stations, in particular, always contained the worst mix of low achievers and degenerates; those who preferred to live a life of petty thievery and piracy outside the long reach of the empire.

She looked again at Constable Dhar, easily recognizable from the picture in his file, which she had studied before coming on board, and tried to decide whether he was feeble-minded, a low-achiever, a degenerate or a mix of all three. On any reputable station or outpost, he wouldn't merit the rank of Constable, which meant he was either here by choice – an easy posting far from the watchful eye of Warfare Command – or he simply lacked the chutzpah to succeed anywhere else.

"Provost Adra, it is a great honor to have you visit our Way Station," Dhar began, adding a little bow and flourish, which only served to make his greeting seem ridiculous and insincere. "We do not see such esteemed officers of Warfare Command out this far very often."

Adra already wanted to throw him over the balcony to the lower level ten meters below, but there was information she needed him to provide first. And she intended to get it quickly, so that she could leave this cesspit of a station at the earliest opportunity.

"I am Constable Dhar and this is my deputy, Nima," Dhar continued, oblivious to the seething hatred burning behind Adra's eyes. "Tell me, how can we serve Warfare Command?"

"I require full access to the security recordings

of the incident, Constable," said Adra, stepping past Dhar and along the gangway towards the staircase that lead down to the main level of docking section seven. She glanced over the railings and saw the Hunter Corvette still docked in front of the constabulary building. "And to interview anyone who came into contact with the criminals that broke onto that vessel and escaped."

"Of course," said Dhar, having to jog to catch up with Adra. Lux and Nima remained a few paces behind them both; Nima attempted to introduce herself, but Lux ignored her and continued marching forwards. "I have already gathered the witnesses in the constabulary," continued Dhar, hoping to impress Adra with his initiative, but his boast drew no reaction from her.

Adra swept down the staircase, drawing nervous looks from the mix of travelers and workers on the lower deck, some of whom quickly vanished into buildings or down corridors. Those that remained made sure to give Adra a wide berth as she stepped off onto the deck and marched towards the constabulary building. She paused briefly in front of the Hunter Corvette, noting that the ramp was still lowered and that a part of it was stained with blood. She turned to Lux, who had carefully followed the direction of her gaze, and he responded without words, moving quickly to take a sample using a device that had been concealed inside his coat. A few seconds elapsed before the analysis was completed, but when it finally appeared on the screen, Lux could not believe his eyes. He looked over to Adra, and his expression seemed to convey all she needed to know.

"Which unit was taken?" said Adra, addressing Dhar, but continuing to observe Lux.

"I don't know, it had no head attached," said Dhar, "They killed two of my militia to get to it, though, and injured more, so it must have been important."

Lux replaced the device inside his coat and then walked up the ramp to access a small console on the wall just inside the cargo bay. Dhar felt compelled to fill the awkward silence that followed, forgetting his own advice to Nima about not volunteering information. "They're probably just racketeers; we get a lot of them out here. Why they decided to go for a simulant, I don't know."

Adra's eyes flicked across to Dhar, and then back to Lux. The more words that came out of the Constable's mouth the more he irked her.

"They took the Casey Valera unit, Provost," said Lux, stepping down from the ramp and back onto the deck. There is superficial damage inside from small arms fire; I have dispatched drones to make the appropriate repairs."

Adra nodded and then continued marching towards the constabulary building. Lux followed, the ramp to the Corvette's rear cargo bay whirring shut behind him.

"We have people who can repair the ship," said Dhar, but Adra ignored him and pushed open the door to the constabulary. Dhar wondered why she did this instead of stepping through the opening created by the smashed exterior glass walls, which still lay in fragments all across the deck. But as the door swung open and clattered against the frame, the drone of chatter and laughter from the militia inside vanished. All eyes were on Adra's imposing, armor-clad frame as she walked into the middle of the room and stopped in front of a desk that contained one of the few remaining working consoles. A haggard-looking male militiaman who was working there quickly scrambled away once he realized Adra was standing above him.

"Provost, we can go to my office, it will..." Dhar began, but Adra cut across him.

"Show me any relevant security feeds on this monitor," she ordered, ensuring her voice was loud enough for everyone in the room to hear, "and bring out those you have detained for questioning."

"Bring them out here?" Dhar asked, and unseen by him or the others, Nima winced. Dhar wasn't stupid, but he also wasn't especially bright, and nor was he following his own eminently sensible advice to not question the Provost. That he was doing so in public only made it worse, and as Adra's hand clenched into a fist, he seemed to realize this just in time. "Yes, I'll do it at once, Provost Adra," Dhar said and then quickly disappeared into the cell block at the rear, forgetting to bring up the security feed on the monitor. To the clear astonishment of the other militia, all of whom would rather be anywhere other than in the same room as a Provost, Nima stepped beside Adra and entered the appropriate commands. She then respectfully backed away and looked down at her hands, which were pressed into a tight bundle in front of her to stop them from shaking. Adra glanced back at the Deputy and studied her for a moment, before returning her attention to the console.

The mood inside the constabulary remained tense as the minutes ticked by, each one feeling like hours to Nima, while Adra quietly studied the security feeds. After an initial cursory scan, she had focused on two feeds, which were displaying on separate monitors. One was of the firefight on the Hunter Corvette and the other was of the confrontation with the racketeers in the Freighter Guild. Adra enhanced two short clips of the feeds, which repeated on a loop on the monitors. The first showed a figure dressed as a Vice Provost on the Hunter Corvette aiming and firing her weapon at the pursuing militia, while the second showed a clear view of the Taylor Ray simulant in the Freighter Guild, using its enhanced strength and reflexes to subdue the racketeers. Adra took a step back and then glanced at Lux, who peered back at her, eyes widened almost imperceptibly, but enough to indicate to Adra that he had seen what she had seen.

At that moment, Dhar bustled back into the room with an escort of militiamen who were herding three prisoners towards Adra. The first was the Guild Master, Goker, the second was Sub-Deck Chief Mallor and the third was Rheyda, the female racketeer with the scarred face. Dhar lined them up in front of Adra, but on the opposite side of the desk to where she stood, and then walked around to join the Provost, standing an arm's length away.

"You will answer the Provost's questions," snarled Dhar, "any lies, and we will know."

Adra looked at the three prisoners in turn. She no longer needed to question them, since the security feeds had already told her everything she needed to know. There was only one question she wanted to ask, the response to which would decide their fates. She turned the monitors to face the three prisoners and their eyes fell onto the images.

"Can you identify these figures?" Adra asked. The brevity of the question seemed to confuse all concerned, especially Dhar, and the three prisoners looked anxiously at each other, wondering who should speak first. Eventually Goker plucked up the courage.

"That is the Vice Provost who came to my Freighter Guild in search of a group of racketeers," Goker said, calmly, volunteering the minimum amount of information he believed he could get away with. Then he nodded in the direction of the female racketeer, "That one there, in fact," he added. Rheyda scowled and started to protest, but one of the militia standing behind her jabbed a truncheon into her back, quickly silencing her objection. "And the other one was her simulant companion."

Though vague, the answer seemed to satisfy Adra, and she redirected her attention to Mallor, who looked about ready to faint. "It is as the Guild Master says, Provost. I am sorry, she wore the uniform and I saw no reason to question her identity..."

"Nor should you have," Adra interrupted, causing Mallor to shrink even further into his own body, but to his relief, Adra next addressed the racketeer. "And you, criminal?"

"I was doing nothing wrong," Rheyda growled, showing none of the respect the others had shown to Adra. "The Freighter Guild is supposed to be the one place in the galaxy where we can get a drink without being bothered by you."

"I apologize for the intrusion into your facility," Adra said, directing the response to Guild Master Goker, whose dumbstruck expression was mirrored by the others, especially Dhar. And while Lux was becoming proficient at hiding his reactions, he too was visibly shocked at hearing the words, 'I apologize' escape the Provost's lips. Adra then returned her attention to the racketeer and repeated her original question, this time with an obvious but carefully controlled malevolence. "Can you identify these figures?"

"It's as they say, a Vice Provost barged in and attacked my crew, and the other one was her simulant puppet," Rheyda answered, sounding bored and bitter. "Those things are also not allowed in the guilds, by the way…"

Adra again did not react to the disrespecting tone and turned to Constable Dhar. "And you, Constable? What is your assessment?"

Dhar's already sickly-pale complexion seemed to lighten still further; he had not expected to also be questioned. "As they say, Provost," he blustered, "though I have never seen a simulant act as that one did; it was almost as if it had independent thought." He paused waiting to see if his answer had satisfied Adra, but she continued to peer down at him, expectantly.

"And what is your explanation for attacking a Vice Provost of Warfare Command?" Adra asked.

Dhar now looked deeply unsettled; in a room full of mercenaries and criminals, it now appeared that he was the one on trial. "Well, there was something not right about her," Dhar blabbed; he had now fully committed himself to ignoring his own rules. "When she was trying to leave the Corvette with the other simulant body, I saw that she seemed to be..." he struggled for the right words, before realizing there were no right words. With barely a handful of sentences spoken, the Provost had trapped him and forced him to reveal all the secrets he had expressively warned his deputy against revealing. "She seemed to be in disguise."

"Disguised as what, Constable?" said Adra, and the sound of her voice was like the snap of a snare closing around Dhar's throat.

"I... I... am not certain," Dhar stammered, "but her skin color was different. If I didn't know better, I'd even say human."

The words barely had time to register in the ears of those in the room before Adra had kicked Dhar in gut with such speed and ferocity that he bent double and collapsed to his knees, unable to breathe. A second later Adra had grabbed the Constable's head and driven her armored knee into it, demolishing bone and cartilage, before she tossed the body on the desk, sending files, drinking cups and empty food containers scattering across the floor. Dhar writhed feebly and helplessly, drowning in his own blood, before Adra sealed his fate by hammering her elbow into his neck and crushing his throat with a single, vicious blow. A deathly silence fell over the room, punctuated only by the dying croaks of Constable Dhar. Adra stood tall, allowing the gravity of her actions to register fully in the minds of all the witnesses, and then she addressed the room.

"Humans are extinct. You all know this," Adra roared. Then she gestured to Dhar's body; the Constable's eyes still showing a glimmer of life. "Constable Dhar failed. He allowed racketeers disguised as a simulant and an officer of Warfare Command – that alone being a crime punishable by death – onto a Warfare Command vessel. He allowed theft of valuable simulant assets. He tried to cover his mistakes with preposterous lies." Then she pointed to Dhar's now still body and her roar grew more ferocious. "This is the price of failure! This is the penalty for dishonesty and disloyalty."

No-one moved. No-one made a sound. Adra turned and met the terrified eyes of Deputy Nima, "You are now in charge of security on this station, Constable Nima," said Adra, though she made it sound like the promotion was more of a punishment than a reward. "Be sure you do not make the same mistakes."

Nima had seen and learned more in the last ten minutes than in two years serving under Dhar, and most importantly of all, she had learned when to keep her mouth shut, which is what she did at that moment. Adra then reached inside her coat and drew a plasma pistol, before wheeling around a full one hundred and eighty degrees and firing a single, precisely aimed shard directly into the forehead of the scarred racketeer, Rheyda. The resulting explosion showered Mallor and Goker with blood and brains and fragments of bone, but neither moved. Neither said a word. Adra returned the pistol to her holster and walked out of the constabulary, with her Adjutant dutifully and wordlessly in tow.

As Lux followed his commander, his mind was fizzing, trying to process what he'd just witnessed and piecing it together with the information he already knew. There was only one conclusion, which was that Adra had been correct all along. There did exist a simulant who possessed independent thought, and who could seemingly interface with the CoreNet. But it was not operating alone. There was at least one human being left alive in the galaxy – his analysis of the blood sample taken from the ramp of the Hunter Corvette had confirmed it beyond doubt – and she must be found and stopped at all costs. Lux drew alongside his Provost, but did not speak and did not alter his expression to suggest any emotion or sentiment. Yet inside he was burning with admiration for Adra's intuition and her decisive action. He had been wrong to ever question her judgment, and he would not do it again.

TWENTY

Sonner opened her eyes, flooding them with a sudden and intense white light that only served to make the throbbing in her temples pulse harder. She squinted and eventually managed to make out a face peering down at her, silhouetted against the searing overhead strip lights. It was the simulant face of Casey Valera, and she was smiling.

"Am I dead?" croaked Sonner.

"Not yet..." said Casey, cheerfully.

"Oh no, I get what's happened. I'm a simulant and this is my awakening, right?" said Sonner, eyes still scrunched tight.

"Yes. You're the Queen Simulant and I am your servant," said Casey. "What is thine bidding Your Majesty?"

"Get me a strong coffee and a fistful of painkillers," said Sonner, pushing herself upright and letting out a single continuous, groan until she was perpendicular. She then realized she was in her quarters and that Casey wasn't the only visitor; Taylor was sitting in her desk chair at the end of the bed, grinning.

"What the hell are you doing in my quarters?"

"Nice to see you too," said Taylor, standing up and checking the dressing on Sonner's head.

"Stop fussing already, I'm fine," said Sonner, batting Taylor's hand away. But then she took a deep breath and smiled. "But thanks for patching me up."

"What's this? Gratitude?" said Taylor, sarcastically, "What have you done with the real Sarah Sonner?!"

"I told you, this is her majesty, Queen Sarah Sonner of the Simulants," said Casey, smirking. "Kneel, and pay homage to your sovereign..."

Taylor played along with Casey's game and dropped to one knee, resting his forearm across it, as if patiently expecting a knighthood.

Sonner rolled her eyes, "Hilarious... I take it since we're not atoms floating in space that you managed to evade that monstrosity of a warship for long enough to jump away?"

"Actually, we have Casey to thank for that," said Taylor, rising again, but still smiling. In fact, he'd been unable to stop smiling since Casey had run rings around the Hedalt frigate; despite the newness of seeing simulant Casey at the helm, there was still something reassuringly familiar about watching her do her thing.

"I see..." said Sonner, peering at Casey with obvious admiration, "In that case, I'm very glad you managed to adjust to your new..." Sonner paused, searching for an appropriate word and settled on, "reality."

"Oh, I'm parsecs distant from being adjusted to whatever this is," replied Casey, gesturing to her own body, "but for some reason, I feel okay with it. Don't ask me how or why, because I don't know, and I'm happy not knowing."

"Good, because we're going to need more of your fancy flying in the future, if you're up for it?"

"Flying is all I ever wanted to do, Commander Sonner," chirped Casey. "I may just be a brain in some fake body, but I know that much is still true. So long as I'm out here amongst the stars, I'm still me."

"Speaking of being out amongst the stars," Taylor said, "we're currently holding position at the edge of the system you directed us to. There are five planets, ten moons, and the biggest damn asteroid belt I've ever seen, and all of it as cold and lifeless as my non-existent simulant heart."

"Aww, Cap, don't say that," said Casey, as if she was comforting a younger sibling, "You're still the same Captain Taylor Ray I remember."

"Technically, we actually only met a few hours ago," Taylor corrected her, "but thanks all the same, Casey, it actually means a lot that you think so."

"I'm sorry to break up such a beautiful and poignant moment..." Sonner interrupted, "but can we move this conversation to the bridge, so you can both get the hell out of my quarters?"

"Sorry, Commander S," said Casey, deciding on a new nickname for Sonner, "we'll let you get dressed and see you out there."

"Get dressed?" Sonner said, hurriedly looking under the sheets and noticing that she was only wearing her undergarments. "Who the hell got me undressed?"

Taylor make a beeline for the door, "Your uniform had blood on it," he commented, before stepping out.

"That doesn't answer my damn question, Captain!" Sonner shouted after him, causing Casey to giggle, but Taylor had already made a swift exit. She shook her head and decided to put the question of who had disrobed her out of her mind, instead turning to more pertinent matters. "Has Taylor explained our situation to you? About why we're out here?"

Casey nodded, "You were out for a good few hours, while we bounced around the Fabric to get here," she answered, "so yeah, he filled me in."

"And you're on-board with it?"

"Like I said, Commander S, all I ever wanted to do is fly," said Casey, "and if we can kick those aliens off Earth along the way, then why not?"

Sonner smiled. "Okay then, I'll see you on the bridge in ten."

"Aye aye, Commander Sarah Sonner," said Casey, before she hopped up and breezed out of the door, red sneakers sparkling like gemstones.

Sonner laughed, suddenly understanding the true origin of Taylor's eclectic acknowledgment of her commands; it had been how Casey had responded to his orders. Despite neither of them technically having met each other before, the core essence of the people they were remained the same, and so did their unique bond. They were part of a team; each a part of something bigger than themselves. She had challenged Taylor's dogged insistence on rescuing Casey, Satomi and Blake, but now she realized just how important it was to find and re-build his entire crew. As individuals they were each skilled, capable, valuable assets to the cause, but as a crew they could be something special. And if they were to win this war, they would need 'special' in spades.

TWENTY-ONE

The shrill tone of the collision warning alarm penetrated the bridge for the sixth time in two minutes, but as on the previous five occasions, Casey Valera deftly steered the nimble Corvette clear of the approaching asteroid, causing the alarm to fall silent.

"I'm going to start hearing that damn squawk in my sleep at this rate," said Sonner, perched literally on the edge of her seat, "and then I'll wake up in a cold sweat, with giant rocks imprinted on my retinas."

Casey glanced back at Sonner and grinned, "I don't know what you mean, this is fun!" she said, and although it was said in an effort to tease Sonner, it was truthful too; Casey was relishing the opportunity to navigate through an asteroid field, especially one as dense and massive as the one she was flying through now. "I'll try to get a bit closer to the next one, if you like? My record is to pass within twelve meters, but I reckon I can probably get it to ten or less."

"Thank you, pilot, but that won't be necessary," Sonner replied, becoming stern and teacherly. "And please can you watch where you're going, young lady?"

"Aye aye, Commander Sarah Sonner," Casey chirruped, returning her focus into the pilot's viewport as another massive asteroid hurtled towards them.

Taylor witnessed the exchange from the mission ops console and chuckled to himself, remembering how he always used to react to Casey's flamboyance with the same passive-aggressive authoritarianism, as Sonner had just done. But, now that the boot was on the other foot, and he was no longer the recipient of Casey's joshing, he saw the humor in it. It also helped that he was familiar with Casey's exceptional piloting skills, which meant that while Sonner was on the verge of falling off her seat and having a nervous breakdown, he had not doubted Casey's ability to navigate the asteroid field for a nanosecond.

Taylor focused back on his console and finished checking the course that Sonner had provided, updating them based on their new navigational data. He then relayed the updated information to Casey's console, before strolling over to Sonner's side.

"If you creep any closer to the edge of that seat, you'll fall flat on your ass," he commented, while standing with his hands behind his back and staring up at the viewport with an imperiousness worthy of Admiral Lord Nelson.

"I swear she's trying to fly closer just to mess with me," muttered Sonner, who was now gripping the arms of the command chair.

"Oh, almost certainly," beamed Taylor, "Get used to it. But, also don't worry; I honestly doubt there's a better natural flyer in the entire galaxy."

The collision alarm sounded again and Sonner held her breath as the ship adjusted course sharply, thrusters pulsing all around the hull of the scorpion-shaped vessel, changing pitch and yaw and altering their trajectory to allow the asteroid to soar past them harmlessly.

"Thanks for the updated data, Cap!" Casey shouted back, while also giving a thumbs up sign, "That last one was close." She then became distracted by a new item of information that had flashed up on her console, and moments later she let out an exuberant whoop. "Nine meters – a new personal best!"

"I much prefer it when she does her flying in the vast emptiness of deep space," said Sonner, after a sharp intake of breath.

"Hey, we're only here because of you," said Taylor. "Whose crazy idea was it to hide a base inside a giant asteroid in the midst of the most chaotic swarm of rocky death the galaxy has ever seen?"

"How should I know? I'm just an engineer," said Sonner, indignantly. "Though you have to admit, on the scale of places the Hedalt are unlikely to look, this ranks only slightly lower than the center of a black hole or the orbit of a blue star."

Casey spun her chair around to face them, red sneakers flashing like lasers, "Yoohoo! Large asteroid ahead!" she called out, before spinning back to grab the controls again. "This one is a real biggie; it's about four hundred Ks across. I reckon it's our guy."

Sonner looked up at the giant asteroid that was rapidly filling the viewport and then glanced down at the console built into the command chair. "It matches the dimensions and composition," she said, "and it's more or less in the right place, accounting for over three hundred years of drift. I'm not picking up any signals, though."

"Would you expect to?" asked Taylor. "The only reason my crew detected the first Contingency base was because of a malfunction that switched on the surface transmitter."

"The plan was for the stasis pods to be revived

after fifty years, remember?" Sonner replied, "If everything had gone to plan then the base should be active, and from this range, I should be getting something."

Taylor moved back over to the mission ops console and conducted some deeper scans, but they only confirmed Sonner's initial assessment. "You're right, that rock isn't emitting any kind of power signature or EM radiation. At least nothing powerful enough to get a reading on from here."

"I've found the cave mouth and I'm heading inside," Casey called out, "switching on the external floodlights. Hold onto your seats!"

Taylor returned to Sonner's side, "You guys like your caves, don't you?" he said, as Casey piloted inside the jagged opening, which was suddenly exposed to five hundred thousand lumens from the ship's front floodlights. The cave structure was wider than the one that led into the lava tube where the first Contingency base was hidden, and at the end of the giant tunnel appeared to be two landing platforms. One was empty, but Taylor's simulant eyes could already make out that the second was not. "There's a ship docked there!" Taylor exclaimed, partly out of surprise and partly from excitement.

Casey approached the second platform and then pointed the nose of the Corvette at the other ship, reducing the intensity of the floodlights so that the image wasn't completely washed out.

"I don't recognize the configuration," said Casey, "Is that an Earth Fleet ship, or does my squishy lab-grown brain just not remember it?"

"No, it's not an Earth Fleet ship, unless my brain is just as squishy as yours, Casey," said Taylor, and then he looked to Sonner for enlightenment, which she duly delivered.

"It's not a military ship, it's a hauler," Sonner explained, "They were used to transport supplies and people to the moon colonies, but during the war some were requisitioned as personnel carriers by the Contingency Council. It was thought they'd attract less suspicion and attention than Nimrods or other military ships."

"So that was the original ship that brought people to this base over three hundred years ago?" asked Taylor, understanding what an affirmative answer would likely mean for the prospect of survivors.

Sonner sighed and stood up; her shoulders were hunched and her face was drawn, like someone who had just failed an exam. "It would seem so."

"Hey, it doesn't mean anything," said Taylor, but with an intentional assertiveness to avoid it sounding like condescension. He knew Sonner was a realist and didn't like anything to be sugar-coated. "You survived for over three hundred years; others can too. Maybe, they just chose not to leave when they didn't receive word from the main Contingency base?"

"Well, let's find out, shall we?" said Sonner, flatly. "Casey, set her down please. I'll see if I can use my command codes to spark up the base's generators and trigger the umbilical; I don't really fancy a spacewalk."

"Aye aye, Commander Sarah Sonner," Casey replied and then began to glide the Contingency One over the landing pad, before setting it down as gently as a parent would a newborn baby. Sonner entered her command codes and a few seconds later, lights surrounding the external dock flickered on and an umbilical slowly extended towards the ship, shaking off centuries of accumulated rock dust as it did so.

"The umbilical is working, so there's still power, which is a good sign." said Taylor, looking at Sonner, but her expression suggested she was not as hopeful as he was.

"The backup power cells could have lasted this long; it doesn't mean that anyone is still alive."

"I'm reading breathable air still, though," Taylor added, enjoying being the optimist out of the two of them for a change. But then he realized how unusual this was. "Could the oxygen generation and processing systems have been running for all this time?"

Sonner continued to look pensive, "Perhaps,

but they shouldn't have kicked back in until the stasis chambers began their wake up cycles. So, it could just be the same air from centuries ago that was trapped inside when they sealed the base up tight."

"Or it could mean there are still people on the base..." Casey joined in, looking on the bright side, as ever. "You never know, there could be new generations of humans in there!"

"I love your positivity, Casey; let's hope so," said Sonner, but then with a more solemn tone, added, "But, since we have just docked in an enemy cruiser, let's not take any chances. I suggest we go in armed, using non-lethal rounds. If anyone is inside, they might shoot first and ask questions later."

"Especially if they see two Hunter simulants coming their way," Taylor agreed, looking at Casey. "Good idea; better safe than shot to pieces."

"I don't think that's how the saying goes, Cap, but I get your meaning..." Casey replied, smiling.

Casey locked down the controls and all three left the bridge, detouring via the armory, where each of them took a sidearm, weapons belt with non-lethal rounds, and body armor.

Casey got half-way through putting the armor on and then stopped. "Force of habit... I guess I don't really need this anymore," said Casey, slipping the vest back over her head.

"No, put in on," said Sonner. "Tin Man or not, if you get shot in the chest and your power systems are damaged, you're just as dead as anyone else."

Casey hadn't considered that. "Wow, okay. I guess I just thought I was invulnerable now."

"Augmented, but not invulnerable," Taylor clarified, "so keep your head down, Casey, same as always."

"Especially your head," Sonner added, "I can fix a lot of things, but an ability to re-grow brains is not on my resume."

Casey nodded and finished strapping on the armor, before they all moved out to the airlock door, slapping the special ammo clips into their weapons and loading them. Sonner operated the controls, while Casey and Taylor waited, weapons raised. Taylor glanced back at Casey and noticed she looked anxious, and then he realized he'd seen this same look before, on the face of his Casey Valera. It was just before they'd entered the Contingency base, before he knew what he was, and before his Casey, Satomi and Blake had been killed.

"Don't worry, you'll do just fine, Casey," said Taylor, knowing that this Casey likely had the same self-doubt. "Better than fine, actually."

She nodded and exhaled heavily, "Thanks Cap, but I haven't actually done this sort of thing before; at least not that I remember," she said, sounding embarrassed by the admission. "I know they're not really my memories, but it still feels like they are."

It was a literal moment of déjà vu and Taylor had to fight back the urge to smile. Casey had nervously admitted to a similar lack of combat experience on the first Contingency base. Back then, his Casey had conducted herself with the composure and bravery of a veteran. He had no doubt that this Casey would perform just as well; other than her choice of footwear, he struggled to tell the difference between them.

"You're better at this sort of thing than you think," said Taylor with calm confidence. "Trust me, I know."

Casey's simulant brow raised up, "That sounds like the beginning of an interesting story…"

"For sure, but one for another time…"

The airlock hissed and began to slide open. Sonner looked at the others and nodded, and then they moved out together into the umbilical. The air and surfaces were damp and cold from centuries of non-use, despite the heater systems having kicked in. They quickly reached the inner airlock door that led into the base and Sonner worked fast to enter her codes. Water droplets fell from the top of the umbilical like rain, making it feel like they were busting into some downtown warehouse on Earth, rather than a base on an asteroid half a galaxy away. A few seconds later the airlock door slid back into its housing and they all got their first look inside the second Contingency base.

"We used to call these sorts of deserted outposts 'ghosts', back when I was still under the influence of the Hedalt's programming," remarked Taylor, peering anxiously into the bleak corridor ahead.

"Not afraid of the dark, are we Captain?" asked Sonner, though in truth, the place was giving her the creeps too.

"Of course not," replied Taylor, sounding offended. But then he paused, and the corner of his synthetic lips curled up slightly. "But, all the same, how about you go first?"

TWENTY-TWO

Sonner rushed through the airlock first and took cover, while Taylor and Casey swept in behind. The Corridor was dimly lit and cold, like an old cave mine, but the air smelled crisp and clean. Sonner waved Taylor forward and he took the lead, moving swiftly up to a junction, before peeking down the adjoining corridors. He signaled the others that the coast was clear and they hurried to join him, weapons held at low ready.

"This air certainly doesn't smell centuries old," Taylor said to Sonner, "I have a feeling that someone is home, after all."

"Agreed," replied Sonner, crouching low beside him with Casey close behind, looking calm and poised. "Hopefully, once they see me, they'll realize this isn't a Hedalt attack."

"All the same, we should expect the worst," said Taylor. "So, assuming we're about the walk into an ambush, where would be the most likely place to set one up?"

Sonner scratched her ear and wrinkled her nose as she thought. "If I remember rightly, down to the right should be a storage and maintenance bay," she jabbed her sidearm along the corridor to Taylor's right, "and to the left are the engineering sub-sections; power, heat, air and water recycling, and so on. I wouldn't want to risk a firefight in there."

"So we go straight down the middle," Taylor replied, agreeing with Sonner's assessment. "Where does that lead?"

"It heads directly into the main concourse of the base," said Sonner. "Honestly, if it were me in there and I just saw a Hedalt Corvette dock, I'd hit us as soon as we walked through the door."

"In that case, you two should go in first," said Casey, her tone and expression flat. Sonner and Taylor looked at her, equally astonished, and then she burst out laughing. "You should see the looks on your faces! I'm just kidding."

"Jeez, Casey, I don't remember you having such a dark sense of humor," said Taylor, relieved.

"Well, you haven't know me all that long, Cap," said Casey, breezily, and then added, "Shall we?"

"Honestly, I don't know what twisted mistake

of fate got me saddled with you two," said Sonner, shaking her head, "but can we reign in the jokes, at least until we're not in imminent danger of dying?"

"Aye aye, Commander Sarah Sonner," said Casey and Taylor, almost in perfect harmony, and then they both looked at each other and laughed. Unusually, Sonner was at a loss for words, and so instead went on ahead, grumbling to herself.

Casey was right, of course; despite the many obvious similarities, there was bound to be more than just her red sneakers that separated this version of Casey Valera from the one he'd known. This should have made Taylor nervous, worrying about whether he needed to second guess himself and question her actions more, rather than trust his memory of Casey, but it didn't. Casey's core personality and instincts were the same, but her different experiences had created a unique individual, in the same way that he was a new and unique Taylor Ray. He knew this Casey as intuitively as he'd know his version, but at the same time he looked forward to discovering more of the idiosyncrasies that made his new friend one of a kind.

Taylor and Casey caught up with Sonner at the end of the central corridor, and moved to the side of the large, manual double doors. The doors were heavily armored and seemed to serve as an additional layer of security and protection against atmospheric leakage from the airlock. Because of this there were no porthole windows, and so they had no idea whether someone was lying in wait for them on the other side.

"Unless anyone has a better suggestion, I say we go in hard and fast," said Sonner, grabbing one of the heavy door handles, "This should open into a wide, two-tier concourse; you two go left, and I'll go right. We take cover behind the closest stone pillars, assess the situation and go from there."

"Sounds like a solid plan," said Taylor, and he glanced at Casey who seemed to agree, or at least to not disagree.

"Okay, on three..." said Sonner, as Taylor took hold of the handle of the other door. "Three... two... one... go!"

Taylor's enhanced strength meant he had no problems in pushing the door open, and within a matter of seconds he and Casey had rushed through and found cover behind a large stone pillar. It was one of many that lined the wide concourse, supporting the structure of the cave, inside which the base had been built. Taylor checked back and saw that Sonner had also scrambled to a similar position on the other side. There was a deathly silence as they all watched and waited, expecting bullets to land all around them, but there was nothing.

"Casey, cover me..." said Taylor, and he moved

out from behind the pillar, quickly advancing to the next, checking all around, including on the upper level. The concourse was dimly lit, like the corridor before it, but the air inside felt warmer, suggesting that the environmental systems on the base were up and running. Yet despite this there was no evidence or suggestion that the base was still occupied. Sonner moved up behind Taylor, but Casey remained, covering them both.

"Looks like no-one is home, Commander..." said Taylor, "at least not anymore." But then he noticed something glinting in the middle of concourse, about ten meters away. He could make out that it was polished metal, but even his simulant eyes couldn't determine precisely what it was from this distance. "Hold on a moment, cover me, I've seen something..." said Taylor, and then he crouch-ran towards the glinting object.

"Captain, what are you doing, get back!" Sonner urged, but Taylor had already gone. Sonner looked over to Casey, who was frantically checking the lower level, her simulant face clearly strained and likely a mirror of her own expression. "Damn it!" she cursed and rushed ahead to take up position behind the next pillar along, checking the new angles for any sign of an ambush.

Taylor knelt down and picked up the polished metal object. Flipping it over he saw that it was an Earth Fleet Lieutenant's rank tab. "What the hell?"

he muttered under his breath.

"Captain, get back now, that's an order!" Sonner commanded, clearly angry and afraid in equal measure. Taylor quickly glanced around the upper level, saw no-one and began to crouch-run back to cover. He made it three steps before the crack of weapons fire shattered the stillness like thunder in the night. Taylor fell forwards as if he'd just been kicked in the back by a horse, and though he felt no pain, he knew he'd taken damage.

"Captain!" cried Casey, and without hesitation she rushed towards Taylor, her simulant legs springing her forwards like an Olympic sprinter. Sonner leaned out from cover and lay down suppressing fire in the direction where she thought the shots had come from, but she couldn't spot his attacker. As quickly as Casey had leapt out, she had dragged Taylor back into cover and propped him up against the wall. "Captain! Captain can you hear me?"

"Yes, I can hear you," Taylor answered. His upper body felt stiffer, though he could still move his torso and arms. "I think I'm okay. Thanks for hauling me out of there."

"Don't mention it, though I don't remember my Captain being so gung-ho... or dumb," said Casey, her human instincts causing her to release a sigh of relief.

"On the first level!" Sonner shouted towards

Taylor and Casey. "Opposite from your position, twenty degrees!"

Casey made sure Taylor was suitably propped up and out of danger and then pressed her sidearm into his hand, "Look after this for me..." she said, before peeking around the huge column of rock and spotting the shadow of a figure, shifting position, clearly still looking for them.

"Look after this," said Taylor, holding up the weapon. "Where are you going?"

Casey didn't answer, and continued to stare up at the shifting shadow. As she did so, she could feel anger building inside her mind. It was a strange and new sensation; the rage that was swelling didn't knot her gut or pulse though her veins, since she had neither, and this made the raw energy of the emotion somehow more manageable. She was able to control it rather than let it control her. It felt empowering and intoxicating; rather than be dominated by her emotions, she could shape them and use them, like weapons. Stepping out from behind the pillar, to the continued shock and astonishment of Taylor, she fixed her eyes on the railings close to where she had seen the shadow. Then she crouched low and using the explosive power contained in her simulant body, propelled herself upwards as if the cold rock floor had been a giant trampoline. Taylor and Sonner could only watch, mouths slightly agape as Casey caught the railings on the second level, almost five meters up from the ground floor and then vaulted them with the grace of a gymnast.

Casey landed in front of the figure, which was no longer a shadow, but a young man, perhaps similar in age to Casey's original human host at the time she was harvested. But he looked more like a cave man, with unkempt, shoulder-length brown hair and a knotted, gingery beard, though paradoxically his clothes were clean and unspoiled. The surprise appearance of Casey leaping over the railings acted like an electric shock, momentarily paralyzing the man. Casey saw the sidearm glinting in his left hand and lunged forward, catching the barrel before he could raise it at her. The weapon fired, but Casey had already aimed it off to the side and the round thudded harmlessly into the wall. Her grip was so powerful that the metal barrel pinched into an oval, before her assailant managed to jerk it out of her grasp and back-pedal frantically, terrified blue eyes peering out at her through the mess of hair. Arm shaking, he raised the sidearm at Casey and fired again, but the round exploded in the barrel. The man howled in pain and threw down the weapon, before falling to his knees, clutching his burned left hand to his chest. Casey advanced and stood over the figure, her own hands curled into fists.

"To hell with you, simulant scum!" the man

yelled, "Go on, do it! Do it!"

"Who are you?" Casey demanded, feeling her anger dissolve now that the threat had been neutralized. But the man kept his eyes turned away, clearly terrified at the sight of her. "Look, I'm not going to hurt you," Casey added, more gently. "I'm not a Hunter simulant. At least, not anymore."

The man chanced a look up at Casey, eyes and body still trembling, "What do you mean, you're not a Hunter simulant anymore? What are you?"

"I'm Casey," said Casey, cheerfully, unbundling her fists and extending an open hand to the man. "Pleased to meet you. What's your name?"

The man was completely thrown by Casey's greeting and the friendly manner in which it was given, considering the aggressive nature of her arrival. He didn't take Casey's hand, but managed to stammer a response. "James..." he said, battling against the agony from his burned hand to get the word out cleanly. Then he slowly shook the hair away from his face and met Casey's eyes fully. "My name is Lieutenant James Sonner."

TWENTY-THREE

Casey quietly observed as sister and brother worked on repairing the damage to Taylor's simulant frame, caused by being shot twice in the back by James Sonner. Taylor's body armor had mostly stopped the rounds, but the impact had still damaged some of his inner workings, causing his simulated muscles to partially lock up. It was nothing that the Sonner siblings couldn't handle, though; 'nothing more complex than hammering a few dents out of the hull', as Sarah Sonner had commented.

While they were finishing up, Casey's mind returned to the moment Sarah Sonner had discovered that her little brother was still alive. She had reached the first floor, panting and out of breath from the sprint, weapon ready, only to see

Casey extending a hand to the fallen enemy and hauling him to his feet. She had initially raised her weapon and was about to issue a challenge, but then she had seen the face of her brother. For a few seconds neither had moved, both believing the other was just a figment of their imagination — an impossibility, a trick of the mind — until they gave in to hope and raced towards each other, meeting in a tight embrace. Casey had smiled as they both repeatedly checked to make sure the other was real and spoke frantic words of relief and joy.

But as Casey watched she was also struck with a sense of sadness; the real Casey had siblings too, but these, like the original Casey Valera, had been murdered by the Hedalt centuries ago, along with most of the human race. She had always enjoyed solitude, and had often sought it out, but even when sailing through the stars light years from Earth, there was always comfort in knowing that her family was at home, and that she would see them again. There was a universe of difference between choosing solitude and having no choice but to be alone, she realized then. Even worse was the reality that she had truly always been alone. The comforting memories of family didn't belong to her; they were just part of the elaborate fantasy the Hedalt had created as a means to control her. Perhaps her love of solitude was just another part of this fabrication, a convenient story to explain why she had volunteered for the Deep Space Recon missions that were really just a pretext for the Hedalt's murderous scheme. In that moment, as she watched brother and sister reunited in love and happiness, Casey Valera resolved that she never wanted to be alone again.

"There, good as new," said James, putting his tool down on the table beside Taylor. "And, sorry again for shooting you."

Taylor pushed himself up and sat over the edge of the table, grabbing his shirt and hurriedly putting it back on; the sight of his bare simulant chest only served to remind him of his inorganic nature. Despite feeling comfortable in his new skin, he hadn't quite got used to the sight of it yet. "No hard feelings; I'm just glad you didn't aim for the head, is all."

"Maybe a few bullets bouncing off that metal skull of yours would do you some good," said Sonner, folding her arms and fixing Taylor with a piercing stare. "Pull a stunt like that again, and the next person to take a shot at you will be me."

"Aye aye, Commander Sarah Sonner," Taylor answered, throwing up a lazy salute.

"Hey, stop stealing my lines!" said Casey.

Taylor finished buttoning up his shirt and slid off the table. "We're going to need some kind of nickname for Sonner number two, here," he said, slapping James on the back, but misjudging the strength of the blow and causing him to stumble forwards clumsily, "We can't call both of you 'Sonner' – that would just get confusing."

"How about S Junior?" said Casey, but James Sonner's scrunched up face indicated that this wasn't his preferred option.

"I'd stick to flying, Casey," quipped Taylor, before turning to Sarah Sonner. "Come on, Commander, you must have had a nickname for him when you two were growing up?"

"Oh no, don't you dare!" said James, wagging a finger at his sister, but the corners of Sonner's mouth had already taken on a wicked curl.

"We used to call him Son-error, because he was always breaking stuff," said Sonner, laughing, and drawing smirks from the others too, except James, who just scowled.

"That was a long time ago!" James protested. "I'm very careful now."

"Well, he just fixed me, so I'd say that name no longer applies," said Taylor, winking at him. "It's not very formal, but how about we just call you James or LT – short for Lieutenant – until we figure something better, or another name presents itself?"

"I'm fine with either, though technically, I'm the only Sonner here," said James, drawing a scowl and wagging finger from his sister.

"Hey, I never took the SOB's last name as my

own," snarled Sonner, "that tradition was way too twenty-first century for me, and you know it..."

James smiled, "That's not what he thought..." he quipped, enjoying the sweet revenge of getting a rise from his sister.

"Just zip it, Junior Lieutenant Sonner, that's an order," snapped Sonner, still pointing her finger at him like a dagger, but James just laughed and held up his hands in surrender.

"Fine, fine, though it's not like you could court martial me if I did disobey, seeing as we're the only two Earth Fleet officers still in existence." Then he bowed his head slightly and his cheeks flushed, "I apologize, Captain Ray and Pilot Valera, I wasn't thinking."

"Don't worry about it," said Taylor, unhurt by the comment, since in essence it was true. "Technically, we're not really Earth Fleet officers at all; I guess you could say we're just distantly related to them."

"Speaking of the others, Lieutenant, what the hell happened here?" said Sonner, switching to 'Commander Mode', and changing the focus of the conversation to deal with the giant elephant in the room, which was why James was the only one out of hibernation stasis.

James seemed to shrink, like a balloon with a slow puncture. "There's only so much I've been able to find out," he said rubbing his rough beard,

"I managed to run a diagnostic on my stasis chamber and discovered some pretty low-level bugs, both in the coding and hardware design. In isolation, none were that problematic, but by some freak of chance the combination caused the wake timer to malfunction and get stuck in a loop."

"The same happened on the main Contingency base," said Sonner, "I never hung around to diagnose my chamber, though. So what else did you find out?"

"Nothing much more than that," said James, shrugging. "I've tried everything, but as you so tactfully pointed out, sis, I'm only a junior tech. I'm lucky my rank and clearance allowed me to order a cup of coffee from the food processor, never mind gaining access to any of the important back-end systems."

"So that's why you haven't woken the others up..." said Sonner, suddenly understanding the fuller picture.

James nodded, "All I could do was try to stabilize the stasis chambers by maintaining the systems and mechanical parts that I could access. Those chambers that were still working, anyway."

"How many?" said Sonner, asking the most important question of all, but also the one she most dreaded the answer to.

"Just over two hundred are still viable," said James, flatly, "Two hundred forty-three failed, before I was revived." Then he looked away and rubbed the back of his neck, before adding, barely louder than a whisper, "I just left them all in their chambers; I didn't know what else to do."

"Hey, don't beat yourself up, little brother," said Sonner, with genuine warmth and affection. Taylor had seen this from Sonner before; an ability to become empathic and sympathetic in an instant, like a cat retracting its claws and suddenly starting to purr. "There's nothing you could have done to help them. I would have done the same as you."

"So how did you get out?" asked Taylor, but then he was conscious that his question seemed more like an accusation and added, "I mean what was different about your stasis chamber?"

"Ironically, it was another isolated malfunction; a genuine one this time," James answered. "The oxygen regulator blocked and so the automatic fail-safes kicked in to prevent me from dying by asphyxiation. That was four years ago."

"Four years?" said Sonner. "You've been alone on this base for four years?" James just nodded.

"But why didn't you leave?" asked Taylor, again unintentionally making it sound like an accusation, though he was very curious to know the answer, "I mean, there's a ship docked outside; why not take it and get away from here?"

James' brow furrowed and his eyes seemed to sharpen. This time the unintentional accusation had registered, and he had gone on the defensive. He squared his shoulders towards Taylor and when he spoke his anger and frustration were barely contained.

"And go where, Captain? Even if I could have piloted that ship on my own, which I can't, I'd not have made it out of the asteroid field. And if by some remote chance I did, the Hedalt would just have hunted me down, using simulants like you!" James realized he'd gone too far, and pressed his eyes shut, before drawing a long breath and letting it out slowly. "I apologize again, Captain Ray; it's just that I've been over this a million times already in my head."

"No need to apologize, James," said Taylor, placing a comforting hand on his shoulder, "I'm sorry if I caused offense."

James rubbed his eyes and face again, though he now appeared much more relaxed, as if this had been something he'd needed to get off his chest for some time. Taylor and Sonner both knew to stay quiet and allow him to build the courage to speak again, and Taylor made sure to lock eyes with Casey and silently convey the need to give him time. Though he couldn't help but see some cruel irony in the fact that a simulant who had recently discovered that his entire existence had been a lie was the one to be comforting a human who'd just got his life back.

"I thought about it, many times," James said, after a tense silence that lasted several seconds. "I wanted to leave. At first, I just told myself I didn't have the command codes to give me access, but I knew where the captain of the ship kept them. It took me months to finally decide to break into his quarters to take them. I don't know how many times I sat on the bridge of that ship and almost left. I got as far as powering up the engines once," he added, with a pathetic-sounding laugh.

"So why didn't you go through with it?" asked Sonner, glancing at Taylor in a way that suggested it was better if she asked the question that they both knew the answer to.

"Because I was afraid, that's why," said James, looking down at his boots, which were shuffling awkwardly on the metal deck, "Earth was gone. The moon colonies were gone... I held out hope that Earth Fleet would rescue me, but when it became clear no-one was coming... well, I resigned myself to staying. "

"As it turns out you were right to do that," said Sonner, cheerfully, "here we are – the cavalry has arrived!"

The sudden and unexpected joke from the usually ice-cold Commander Sonner was effective at lifting the fog of gloom that had descended over them all.

"You're lucky I didn't blow the docking

umbilical while you were still inside," said James, after he'd stopped laughing, "I only didn't because I figured maybe if I could steal a Hedalt ship, I could jump around without raising suspicion. Maybe find a nice little planet to settle down on, far enough away from the empire to be safe."

"I doubt there's anywhere their hand can't reach," said Sonner with an acid tone, but then her eyes brightened again, "but, thanks for not blowing us into space. I would not have forgiven you for that."

"You were always the one in need of forgiveness, not me, sis," said James, smiling, "Especially from Mom."

"Ooh, that sounds like a story!" said Casey, who had been silently observing until that point, but felt like the opportunity had presented itself to help blow the fog of gloom away fully. "Little girl Commander S was a troublemaker, is that what you're saying?"

"Commander Sonner does not wish for such matters to be discussed," said Sonner, looking down her nose at Casey. "Besides, we have more important matters to attend to."

"What do you have in mind?" asked Taylor, curious as to the meaning of her cryptic response.

"We have just over two hundred Earth Fleet engineers to wake up, of course," Sonner replied.

"Like I said, sis, I don't have access," said James.

"You may not, but I do," said Sonner. "In the event of catastrophic losses in the chain of command, full authority passes to the next most senior command rank officer." Sonner waited for the others to catch on, but Taylor, Casey and James just stared back at her blankly. "Oh, for heaven's sake, me!" she added, throwing her arms up. "But, you don't have to call me Grand Admiral, at least not yet."

"Admiral, Commander, Supreme Overlord... I don't care what you call yourself," said Taylor, "If you can wake up this sleeping crew and get them back to the main base, we may actually have the beginnings of this Contingency you speak of."

"I can wake them up easily enough," said Sonner, "but getting them back to the Contingency base is going to require a very special kind of pilot."

Casey pressed her hand to her hip like a teapot handle and beamed at them, "Did someone say my name?"

TWENTY-FOUR

The process of reviving the two hundred and seven surviving occupants of the base was a slow and laborious one. After over three hundred years in deep hibernation, many were too weak to function and required a period in the medical bay, being prodded and probed and injected with a cocktail of drugs that would get them back on their feet and moving. Due to the limited space and capabilities of the equipment in the rudimentary asteroid base, the revivals were done in groups of twenty, over several days. This was far longer than Sonner would have preferred, though it at least gave everyone time to recuperate and reflect on the challenges that still lay ahead.

The most immediate of these challenges was recovering the group of engineers back to the main

Contingency base, deep inside the lava tube. Sonner had hinted at a plan for this, but they had all been so pre-occupied with reviving the initial crew members, and dealing with their physical debilitation and mental shock at learning the truth of their situation that it had not been discussed further. However, with enough of the base crew now sufficiently compos mentis enough to take over the revival operation, Sonner had called Taylor, Casey and a freshly clean-shaven James together to go over her idea.

Sonner was waiting for them in the empty mess hall, sitting patiently at a circular table with three other chairs already set out. A cup of black coffee sat steaming in front of her. Every other chair in the hall was turned upside down and placed on top of the other tables; all except for one. In the far corner of the mess hall, Taylor could see a single lonely chair neatly tucked underneath a small table for one. He glanced at James and wondered how he'd managed to stay sane living alone for so long.

"Once all the crew are revived, we have just enough capacity between the Contingency One and the hauler outside to get everyone back in one trip," Sonner began, once everyone had sat down. Though it was clear to everyone there was a 'but' coming, and she didn't disappoint. "But, the hauler doesn't have a black market transceiver, like our Corvette, which means it won't be able to jump along the threads."

"Can we blind jump it back?" asked James, but Sonner shook her head.

"It's too far, and we'd still need to make the jump calculations. The computer on that ship has nav data that's three hundred years out of date."

"Could the Contingency One make the calculations for it?" asked Taylor, but this time Casey shook her head.

"No dice, I'm afraid, el Capitan," said Casey, practically singing the words. "The bridge on the Contingency One may look like a Nimrod, but the tech is Hedalt and it doesn't play nice with Earth Fleet gear, I'm afraid."

"That's all beside the point," said Sonner, clearly irritated by the interruptions. "At some point the hauler will have to link to the CoreNet to jump, and when it does, Hedalt Warfare Command will most likely be able to detect it."

"Right..." said James, finally understanding the crux of the problem. "And the last thing we need is for the Hedalt to pick up a three-hundred-year-old Earth Fleet hauler bouncing around inside the Fabric."

"You mentioned needing a hell of a pilot," said Taylor, recalling their earlier conversation, "So you obviously have something in mind?"

Sonner took a slurp of coffee and then nodded and smiled at Casey, "If we can pilot the hauler close enough to the Contingency One and boost its transceiver signal to envelop the hauler, I think we can jump them both and make it look like one ship."

"Just how close are we talking?" asked Taylor.

"If I can boost the transceiver power enough, maybe five or ten meters," said Sonner, drawing a synchronized doubtful raising of eyebrows from the others, including Casey.

"That's crazy," said Taylor, "even a small error in jump piloting could mean the two ships end up blended together after the jump."

"Like I said, we'll need one hell of a pilot," said Sonner, answering Taylor's question, but looking hopefully at Casey.

Casey Valera thought for a moment, puckering up her lips as she did so, and then shrugged, "I can do it, but I'll need control of both ships," she said, sounding only quietly confident, which for Casey was the equivalent of pessimism. "Can you hook up the pilot's viewport on the Corvette to the one on the Hauler?"

Sonner looked at her brother, who took the cue to answer, "Yes, though wouldn't it be easier to just pilot from the bridge of the Hauler?"

"I'll still need control of the Corvette to synchronize their positions," Casey answered, "So I'd rather do it from the pilot's console on the Contingency One; it's just more comfortable, like a well-worn pair of sneakers."

James glanced down at Casey's red footwear and smiled, "Hey, sis, can I get some of those?", but Sonner just shushed him.

"Why did you guys make it so difficult to transport these engineers back to the main base, anyways?" said Casey, spinning her legs out from under the table and wiggling her feet at James, showing off her flashy footwear.

"The plan was never to transport them back to the main Contingency base," said Sonner, momentarily distracted by the flashing of red on the other side of the table. She glanced at Taylor as if expecting him to do something about his officer's behavior, but Taylor just smiled and shrugged, drawing another eye-roll from Sonner. "Had the Contingency worked smoothly, this second base was intended as a hidden repair station for the ships in the Nimrod Fleet. We located it away from main Contingency base so as to reduce the risk of that being detected, and also to provide a location closer to Earth for essential fleet repairs."

"That's why there are only engineers here," James added, semi-entranced by Casey's waggling feet, "and only one beat-up old ship."

Sonner nodded, "The main Contingency base has its own compliment of engineers; or at least it did have."

"It still has one," Taylor added, and Sonner conceded the point with a casual flourish of her hand.

Casey stopped waggling her feet and slid them back under the table. "Okay, so Commander S boosts the transceiver, Sonner number two uses his tech smarts to hook up my pilot's viewport to the hauler, and we jump out of here like one happy family, right?"

"That's the plan," said Sonner. "I like how you make it sound so easy, Casey."

"It's a special talent of mine," beamed Casey and everyone, including Sonner, laughed.

"There's one more thing," Sonner added, after the laughter had faded, "I suggest we leave a couple of sentinel probes behind, to guard the base in case of unwanted visitors."

Taylor frowned. "Do you really think anyone would find it?" Then a different, more pertinent question popped into his head, "And what would it matter; we're never coming back here, right?"

"I hope we never have to come back," said Sonner, but there are so few safe havens for us in the galaxy, I wouldn't want to completely abandon any of them. And after our adventures at the Hedalt space station, I imagine this ship is now on a galaxy-wide 'most wanted' list. If Provost Adra and her War Frigate do manage to catch our scent, it may lead her here."

Taylor nodded, "Fair point. So we keep this place on lockdown, just to be on the safe side."

"I'll sort out the sentinels, I brought some with us from the main base." Sonner downed the rest of her coffee and placed the cup back down on the table with solid clunk. "We all have work to do, so let's get to it."

Sonner adjourned the meeting and they all went their separate ways. James went to the hauler to hook up the ship-to-ship telemetry, while Sonner left for the Contingency One to work on boosting the transceiver signal. Casey decided to spend the time using the simulator mode that was built into the pilot's viewport to practice the dangerous jump maneuver she'd made sound simple. The only person left without an immediate role was Taylor. Initially, he thought to assist with the revival operation – even though the other human crew members were still more than a little wary of a simulant in their midst – and set off in the direction of the stasis chambers and med lab. But he was also distracted; Casey's comment about 'one happy family' had again set him thinking about his own life, and about Satomi, and whether he would be able to reach her again. He stopped and turned back, heading towards the airlock and the umbilical that led back to his ship and his empty quarters. Unlike the main Contingency base, the asteroid didn't cut off the signal from the

CoreNet, which meant he'd still be able to dial in.

Let's see if I can make another phone call, he mused to himself. *I just hope she's still on the other end of the line...*

TWENTY-FIVE

Taylor hurried into his quarters and activated the regeneration mode on the bed that Sonner had engineered out of the original, far more clinical apparatus that had been there previously. The timetable to leave the asteroid base had been stepped up, so he didn't have long, but he wanted to try to reach Satomi, if only for a minute or two.

He lay down and closed his eyes, and within seconds the neural interfaces in his brain had created a link to the regeneration tech in the bed, projecting his consciousness into the deep space corridor. Directly ahead of him was the starlight door and he wasted no time in rushing through, stepping from the confined, safe space of his own thoughts and memories and into the CoreNet. He stopped a few paces beyond the threshold, again mindful that he didn't have much time. He hoped that he might somehow be able to summon Satomi to him, rather than race out into the cosmos to find her, but he had no idea if that was even possible. There was no tech manual describing how to operate the link, and for someone who liked process and procedure, 'winging it' was not really in his nature.

He closed his eyes and took a breath, before trying to focus on Satomi's face. *If you can hear me, follow the sound of my voice...* Taylor said in his mind, but even without hearing the words back, he realized how corny it sounded. "Damn it, Taylor, you sound more like her damn therapist," he admonished himself. "Come on, I should have this figured out by now..."

He took another deep breath and tried again to picture's Satomi's face, which was sometimes easy and sometime almost impossible to remember, no matter how hard he tried. This time, he could see her as clearly as he could see the glowing, wire-framed cubes that extended throughout the cosmos all around him. The clarity of her image in his mind was shocking and almost too much for him to bear. It only reminded him of what he'd lost.

They're looking for you...

"Satomi?" He wasn't sure if he'd imagined the voice. There was no response, but Taylor felt a sudden dull ache inside his head. He rubbed his temples and tried again.

They'll find you... They'll draw you to them. Get out, get out while you can!

"Who will find me?" Taylor shouted. Her voice was strange and ethereal, and though it was clearly Satomi, she sounded almost trance-like.

The pain in Taylor's head started to build, and before he could call Satomi's name again, he felt himself being pulled away, as if lassoed by an invisible rope. He struggled against the pull, but it was no use, and it continued to draw him away from the deep space corridor. Feeling panic rise inside him he twisted and stared at the starlight door, remembering that resistance in this place was an act of the mind, not the body. He focused on trying to get back to the door, reaching out towards it as much with his thoughts as with his desperate, outstretched hands. His progress was slow and painstaking, but eventually he overcame the invisible force. Grabbing the inside of the starlight door frame, he pulled himself through, and then immediately once he was on the other side the strange force on his body vanished, as if the rope had been abruptly severed.

"What the hell?" Taylor peered through the door. He had felt this pull before, the first time he had entered the Fabric and encountered the humanoid aliens on their warship. But this was different; this felt more deliberate. 'They're looking for you,' Satomi had said. She was attempting to warn him. *But who is looking for me?* Taylor wondered. *The Provost?*

He shook the questions from his mind, because more than anything he was angry. He'd managed to reach Satomi, or rather she had reached him, but he'd not had chance to speak to her and the fact he'd come so close was frustrating. He considered going back through the door and trying again, but he resisted the urge, knowing that he should get back to the base and rejoin the others. But as soon as he got the opportunity again, he would return. Whether the Hedalt were truly looking for him or even able to find him inside the Fabric, he did not know, but he did know that nothing was going to stop him from finding Satomi Rose. No warship or Provost or even armada would get in his way, because Satomi was family.

TWENTY-SIX

The collision alarm rang out on the bridge of the Contingency One, forcing Casey to make a series of quick adjustments, and relay the updated course through the asteroid field to the trailing hauler. The bigger, clunkier ship had already taken a series of minor hits since departing the asteroid base, but Taylor had managed to destroy most of the more threatening asteroids with the aft turret. Sonner had advised against shooting apart the bigger hunks in case it just made more targets, so Casey's dazzling piloting skills were still very much needed.

"Cap, there's a mid-size rock heading our way," said Casey, calmly, eyes enveloped inside the pilot's viewport. "I can avoid it, but that slug behind us probably won't."

"Got it, Casey, just give me a moment," said Taylor, trying to target the asteroid, but the entire belt was saturated with EM radiation, and locking onto the soaring boulder was like trying to tune an old FM radio to a distant transmitter.

Casey weaved between a cluster of larger asteroids, and slotted into a new course that avoided the hurtling lump of rock, but the Hauler, as predicted, had been unable to match Casey's maneuvers. "Any time now, Cap, or that slug out there is gonna get squished..."

Taylor locked onto the asteroid and then lost the signal again. Swearing, he switched to fully manual, and brought up the targeting reticule in his tactical console. He'd never been a great shot, but he was hoping his simulant nerves of steel would give him the edge.

"Cap..." called out Casey with a genuine sense of urgency, just as Taylor fired a burst from the aft turret. Seconds later the asteroid fragmented and the smaller chunks flew off in a chaotic spread, two or three bouncing harmlessly off the hull of the hauler as it ploughed onwards.

"See, nothing to worry about," said Taylor, doing his best to sound cool. He took his hands off the targeting controls and looked at them. If he had been human, they would have been shaking like jelly, but they were completely still. This was a rare moment when he thanked his simulant body, because a fully human Taylor Ray would most likely have bungled the shot, putting an end to the contingency war then and there.

"Good shot, Captain!" exclaimed Sonner from the command chair. "But let's try to get our good shooting done a little quicker next time..."

Taylor shot her a casual salute and then pushed out of the chair and hustled up beside Casey just as the Contingency One emerged from the asteroid field, closely followed by the heavily dented and scraped hauler, full of Earth Fleet engineers. "Great flying, as always," he said, gently patting Casey on the shoulder, "I'll double-check the jump program from mission ops. We might actually pull this off after all."

"Aye aye, Captain Taylor Ray," Casey sang, as she flipped a sequence of switches to power up the main engines and jump drive.

Taylor had barely made it two steps towards mission ops when the tactical console bleeped urgently; he didn't need a real stomach to get a sinking feeling. He watched as Sonner anxiously read the alert on her console in the command chair, and saw her complexion whiten and face harden like granite.

"We're picking up two ships emerging from the edge of the asteroid field," Sonner announced, "they match the configuration and markings of two vessels we scanned while docked on the Way

Station." She looked over to Taylor and added, "It appears that our criminal friend, Rheyda, may have figured out we conned her..."

Taylor dashed back to his station and brought up the full tactical scans of the two ships.

"If that's true then they're somehow managing to track our transceiver," said Taylor as the scan data began to flash up on his screen.

"Perhaps a tracer beacon," Sonner agreed, tapping some commands into her console. "I'll have our little repair drones scour the device and disable the tracker. In the meantime, what are we dealing with out there?"

Taylor finished analyzing the tactical scans, "Modified light freighters... well-armed... easily a match for us." Then he looked over at Casey, "Can we jump?"

"They'll be on us before I can get into position with the hauler," said Casey, gravely, "Unless the hauler blind jumps on its own, but that would be like shooting up a flare for the Hedalt to see."

Taylor estimated that the racketeer ships were barely a minute away; whatever they were going to do they had to do it fast. He spun the chair around to face Sonner who was sat like a statue of a Greek philosopher, with a face that was just as stony. She was weighing up a choice that would ultimately affect the success or failure of the entire Contingency.

"If we let the hauler blind jump, this will all be for nothing," Sonner said, looking up at Taylor, "Can you take them out?"

Taylor glanced at Casey; there was not a glimmer of mischief in the pilot's expression any more, just a steely determination, "If you can shoot them, I can make sure we don't get hit," she said, and then paused before adding, with a very slight hint of mischief, "that often…"

Taylor couldn't help but smile. He looked back at Sonner. "Order the hauler to turn back and hide out in the fringe of the asteroid field."

"But they'll get pulverized!" countered Sonner.

"They'll get pulverized out here, but their hull can take asteroid impacts better than it can withstand plasma shards."

Sonner nodded, "That means two versus one, Captain – tell me you're that good?"

Taylor spun the chair around and powered up all the weapons systems to maximum. "We're about to find out… Casey, work your magic."

"Aye aye, Captain Taylor Ray…."

The Contingency One surged towards the two advancing racketeers, while the hauler thrust in the opposite direction and sank back inside the asteroid belt, under Sonner's orders. The panel on the command chair bleeped and Sonner saw that they'd received an incoming communication request; she put it on the main speakers for everyone to hear.

"I am Chodah. Power down and surrender to me or be destroyed," said a male voice.

Sonner slipped back into her Hedalt military character. "How dare you threaten a ship of Warfare Command, under the control of Vice-Provost..."

"Spare me the lies, human, we know who you are," said Chodah, making his disgust clear. "You cost us valuable merchandise, and got Rheyda killed. Your ship, plus the bounty we'll demand from Provost Adra for your human head, is compensation owed to us."

"There will be no bounty if you destroy us," said Sonner, attempting to call their bluff.

"If we have to, we'll settle for your little companion, skulking in the asteroid field," the voice replied, "Your choice, human." Then the comm link went dead.

"Well he was rude," said Casey, sounding genuinely affronted. "Cap, get ready on the forward cannons..."

"What are you going to do?" asked Taylor, hovering his hand over the weapon controls, but he didn't need Casey to answer, because at that moment she kicked the main ion engines into a short, high-powered burst, rocketing the Corvette through the dead center of the two racketeer ships, before spinning it around and decelerating with equal ferocity. The maneuver was executed with such precision that it instantly turned hunted into hunter, putting them directly on the tail of their attackers.

"Firing!" shouted Taylor, quickly locking onto the closest ship and firing a volley from the forward cannons, but the racketeer ship had already begun to evade, and sent out a spread of countermeasures, causing the cannon rounds to explode twenty meters from the hull. The resulting shock wave was still enough to push it into a spin, giving them valuable seconds to focus on the second racketeer.

"Coming about on the second ship," Casey called out, as she angled the nose of their nimble Corvette at the enemy vessel and matched its velocity. But before Taylor could fire, a streak of red energy lashed out from the rear of the racketeer ship and slammed into their dorsal armor. Alarms shrieked on the bridge and Sonner quickly silenced them.

"Damage to the port aft quarter, but we're okay!" she shouted out, "They're firing again!"

This time Casey was ready, and the red beams of plasma flashed past under their belly. At the same time Taylor streaked explosive rounds across the back of the racketeer ship from the dorsal cannons, and a dozen micro-explosions erupted on its hull.

"Damn, that thing has a thick skin!" cried Taylor, as he watched the status of the forward cannons, waiting for them to reload.

"The first ship has recovered and is heading this way," Sonner called out, "Casey, do you see it?"

"A little busy here Commander S," said Casey, as she dodged yet another volley of plasma shards, the last of them glancing off the hull and leaving a scorch mark, like a lightning bolt. "Cap, I'm lining it up!"

"Just another second," shouted Taylor, tapping the status indicator with his forefinger, willing it to turn green. There was an explosion and the ship was rocked like a dinghy riding rapids. Casey's feet and hands moved almost too fast even for Taylor's silver eyes to see, as she threw the Corvette around. "They're dropping grav mines!" she shouted, "I won't be able to stay on their tail for much longer!"

Taylor's finger tapping eventually paid off and the panel turned green; he locked on and fired. Moments later they were pushing through the fiery remains of the racketeer ship, debris bouncing off their hull like giant hailstones.

"Great shot!" Sonner cried out, but then the ship was buffeted again, and conduits exploded, flooding the bridge with acrid, black smoke. Sonner coughed and frantically worked the panel on her chair, running damage control as best she could, but without a full crew, there wasn't much she could do.

Casey spun the Corvette around and powered them in a sharp arc away from the second ship, which fired another volley of plasma shards that narrowly missed their main engines.

Taylor brushed charred debris off his console and read the status. "Cannons are down; all we have are the dorsal turrets," Taylor called out.

"They don't have the punch to penetrate their armor," Sonner replied, coughing violently as the bitter fumes entered her lungs.

"They will if I get close enough," Casey called out, powering the scorpion-like starship low underneath the racketeer vessel, and then doubling back in a maneuver that was as dizzying to experience as it must have been for the racketeer ship to watch. "Five seconds, Captain. They won't fall for this again if you miss..."

Taylor watched in horror and amazement as the belly of the racketeer ship grew rapidly larger on the viewport, "What the hell, Casey, we need to shoot them not ram them!"

"You do the shooting and I'll do the flying!" Casey shouted back, as the enemy ship desperately tried to re-orient itself so that it could get another shot off. If Casey mis-timed by just a second, the racketeer would be able to hit them point blank and turn them to ash. "Now!" she shouted and then stopped the Corvette barely twenty meters from the gut of the enemy ship. Taylor had to fight the human instinct to shut his eyes and shield his face, and engaged the dorsal turrets, which drilled into the racketeer's hull like a demonic woodpecker. Sparks and electrical arcs engulfed the viewport as Casey drew back and the full scale of the damage to the enemy ship became apparent. Its engines flickered and faded as it listed out of control towards the asteroid field.

Sonner rubbed the smoke from her eyes and staggered forward, grabbing the back of Casey's chair, "Did we get it?"

Taylor checked his console, probing the racketeer ship with another barrage of scans, "It's disabled and listing; no engines, no weapons and sensors are down. It's no threat."

"And what about us?" Sonner said, wiping black mucus onto her shirt cuff.

"We're going to need a lick of paint when we reach the Contingency base," said Taylor, reading the updated damage report, "but we can still make it back, assuming Casey can manage another incredible feat of piloting today."

They both looked over at Casey Valera for confirmation, but she was leaning back in her chair, red sneakers resting on top of her console, playing with the wrapper of the mint that Taylor had slipped into her pocket. She caught Taylor and

Sonner looking at her out of the corner of her silver simulant eye, and stared back at them, quizzically. "Did you guys say something?"

TWENTY-SEVEN

The whine of the War Frigate's jump engines descended and was replaced by the untiring, rhythmic beat of the ship's colossal main drives. Provost Adra patiently endured the agony that penetrated every muscle and nerve ending in her body, until it too began to diminish, and then she looked up at the new star system through the main viewport. The tracking beacons planted on the racketeer ships had led them here, though to Adra it appeared to be just another barren and lifeless star system, with the only remarkable feature being that it was sliced into two halves by a vast asteroid field.

After departing from the Way Station, Adra had moved her frigate away from the city in space, but remained close enough to monitor the comings and goings of starships from within its rotten insides. For days she had waited and watched, but eventually her persistence and patience had paid off, as two racketeer ships departed, both jumping together, deep into the uncharted regions of space. Neither were aware that during her time on the station, Adra's simulant automatons had planted tracking beacons onto their hulls. Their direction would provide no occasion for piracy or other criminal endeavors, hence Adra's suspicion that they were in pursuit of the imposters who had posed as Hedalt military and stolen their contraband.

Adra peered up at the array of displays circling above her head, swiping from one to the next, scouring the screens for the information she was hungry to find. And then she saw it; a faint signal, but with the same characteristics as the anomaly they had detected previously. The anomaly she was now certain was caused by the rogue Hunter simulant. It had entered the Fabric again, and as before their purge had failed. But although she was still unable to trace its precise origin, she knew it originated from within the blind jump range of the system they had just tracked the racketeers to. Others may have considered it mere coincidence, but Adra knew better. The human female and rogue simulant had been here – she was certain of it – and she was determined to discover why.

Adra pointed to a screen and then drew her hand towards her chest, balling it into a fist as she did so, and waited for it to swoop down from its perch on the end of its spindly metal arm. She read the scan data and sent the location of the tracking beacon to the pilot's console, where Adjutant Lux was standing, waiting for orders.

"The beacon is located on the edge of the asteroid field," said Adra, "set a course."

Lux peered down at the console and saw the new co-ordinates flash up. Without hesitation, he tapped the primary pilot simulant on the shoulder with the back of his hand, and it immediately set to work, powering up the War Frigate's massive engines and cutting a path through space towards the asteroid field.

"I am detecting debris," said Lux, surveying the new data that was coming in as the frigate drew close to the edge of the asteroid belt. "And one ship, just inside the fringe of the asteroid field. It appears to be disabled and listing, though life support systems are functioning and there are repair drones on the hull."

"Ensure its engines and weapons systems are destroyed and send out tug drones," ordered Adra. "Bring it alongside. I want to speak with them personally."

"Yes, Provost Adra," said Lux and then he went to relay the orders to the appropriate stations and simulant crew. There were brief flashes on the view port as the frigate carefully picked off the weapons on the racketeer ship with highly focused plasma shards, before a succession of flashes rendered the smaller ship's engines inert.

Adra returned her attention to the screen at her right side, broadening the scan radius by a hundred kilometers from the location of the debris field. *If they followed the rogue Hunter Corvette here then why?* she asked herself, her penetrating stare scouring every last centimeter of the screen, looking for anything that might suggest what it was about the system that was important. But, there appeared to be nothing remarkable about it, beyond the unusual size and density of the asteroid field. *What are they doing? What are they hiding?* And then it struck her. *Hiding... Did they hide something here during the war?*

"Launch probes into the asteroid field," Adra called over to Lux, "Have them survey the field using this location as the center point."

"I have already plotted a search plan, Provost," Lux answered, turning to face the command platform. Adra's expression gave nothing away, though she was impressed at his intuition. "But because of the size of the asteroid field and the drift of the debris, it could take weeks to map even this small area."

"Understood," said Adra, as the dull thump of

the docking clamp reverberated through the deck plating. She glanced up at the screens circling overhead and saw that the tugs had successfully retrieved the racketeer light freighter, which was now securely in the grasp of the War Frigate's underbelly, like prey held in an eagle's talons.

"We have the racketeer ship," Lux confirmed, "I have assembled a simulant boarding squad at the airlock. They await your order."

"Command them to hold," said Adra without delay, before stepping off the command deck and marching to the exit, "We will go personally; I want at least one of the racketeer scum taken alive for interrogation."

Lux nodded and then joined his commander. Only a few days earlier he would have felt obliged to advise Adra that personally boarding the racketeer ship was too great a risk; as Adjutant, his job was also to act as personal bodyguard. But his earlier reticence to blindly obey Adra's commands had been replaced by an unswerving confidence in her abilities and intuition. More than that, she was on to something big – the pursuit of a potential new human threat. If she was right, and if they were successful in exposing and even eliminating the threat, it would be a victory that would cement his name alongside hers.

They walked together in silence along the long central vein of the War Frigate, branching off to descend into the heart of the powerful ship. As they approached the airlock gate, a squad of simulants — each covered in a jet-black cocoon of black armor with a smooth, oval face mask — filed in behind them holding deadly plasma rifles. Lux drew back his long black coat at the waist and removed his own plasma pistol, patiently watching Adra to ensure she also armed herself. But instead of drawing her sidearm, Adra reached inside her coat and unsheathed an onyx-black knife with a seven inch blade and sharply-contrasting serrated silver edge. It glinted as she adjusted her grip on the handle, and then she lowered the weapon to her side, its tip angled forwards like the sting of a giant scorpion.

The simulants lined up in three rows of three and Adra and Lux both took up positions behind them, using their combined mass as a shield. Without the rhythmic thud of the simulants' boots, only the hum of the energy surging through the conduits was audible over the stillness that now fell over the airlock gate.

Adra tightened her hold on the blade and issued the command, "Open the door."

No sooner had the airlock begun to slide back into its housing, than a volley of plasma fire surged through the narrow opening, and two of the front rank of simulants fell instantly. The remaining simulants charged forward, firing into the gloom, while Adra and Lux followed behind, standing tall and marching imperiously, as if they were immune to the danger ahead. This was the truest test of a Hedalt soldier's nerve – to confront death without fear, so as to strike fear into the hearts of those that challenge you. Lux knew he was being judged by Adra, but this time he also knew he would not falter.

They both broke through onto the racketeer ship, stepping over the smoldering bodies of five racketeers. Ahead they could see four more, scuttling back towards the bridge while firing frantically at the simulants. A shard of plasma flashed past the simulant blockade and hit Adra on the shoulder; Lux could smell her seared flesh, but Adra did not flinch and did not waver. A racketeer fell as a volley of purple plasma burned holes in her chest and neck. Solid rounds from more primitive weapons ricocheted off the deck and Lux felt an intense heat sting his left thigh, but he clenched his teeth and pressed on, moving through the narrow door and onto the bridge. There were now only three racketeers remaining, and each one was standing with their hands thrust into the air in surrender, surrounded by simulant soldiers, some of whom smoldered like charcoal embers from damage they'd taken during the assault.

"Stand down," commanded Adra, and the simulants obeyed, retreating to the perimeter of the bridge and lowering their weapons. The three remaining racketeers looked to one another, not understanding what was happening and why they were not already dead. "Which of you is the Captain?" Adra continued.

"Our Captain was Rheyda," snarled the racketeer in the center of the three, "you killed her, Provost Adra." Though provost was a rank of high status in the Hedalt empire, the racketeer spat out the word as if it was an insult. "I am Chodah, her brother."

"You may yet be spared your sister's fate, providing you tell me everything you know about the Hunter Corvette you pursued here," Adra answered, indifferent to Chodah's disclosure; he was nothing to her, just as his worthless sister was.

Chodah laughed and then spat a blood-smeared glob of saliva onto the deck in front of Adra; a sliver of the mucus splashed onto her boot. "That's all you'll get from me," he said, defiantly. "And we've already purged our data banks, before you look there."

Lux stepped to a nearby console and began cycling through the systems. The heat of the bullet wound had now turned to a penetrating throb, but he fought back the anguish, despite each step feeling like a knife had been pressed into his flesh. "It is true, Provost, they have purged the data records."

Adra smiled. She despised the racketeers, but allowed herself to feel a grudging respect for their gall and composure in the face of certain death. "You will tell me sooner or later, Chodah," said Adra, relishing the prospect of an interrogation. "I suggest you choose sooner; your death will be less painful if you do."

To her surprise the lead racketeer laughed again. "Soon you will have bigger problems to contend with than us," he said, appearing to enjoy sparring with Adra. "Or did you really believe we had not already called for assistance?"

Lux switched the console display to an external sensor feed, working quickly but calmly so as to show no fear or hint of anxiety. Two new contacts registered on the feed, still at the edge of the system but closing rapidly. Lux knew that Adra had not informed Warfare Command of their whereabouts, since their mission was not sanctioned, which meant that the readings confirmed Chodah's gloat that they had help on the way. He returned his hand to his side and looked at Adra. To the racketeers, Lux's expression revealed nothing – it was blank and impenetrable, like the visors of the simulant soldiers – but Provost Adra understood its meaning, and her grip on the blade tightened.

"Soon, you will be our prisoner," Chodah bragged, "and then we will see how strong you really are, Provost, without these abominations to protect you."

Adra was like a grenade with a lit fuse; she held the contemptuous stare of the lead racketeer and spoke a single word. "Withdraw."

Immediately, the simulant soldiers filed off the bridge of the ship, before grouping together in the corridor outside and marching away. The three racketeers watched in stunned silence, again unable to fathom the actions of the Provost, who seemed utterly unfazed by the departure of her protectors. It was now three against two, and the racketeers could all see that Adra wielded only a blade.

"You're a fool if you think we won't kill you," said Chodah, muscles taught.

Adra's eyes narrowed and then she raised the blade towards them as if it were a dueling sword. "You can try."

One of the other racketeers darted off from the group and grabbed a rifle that had been discarded onto the deck. He raised the weapon and then a flash of purple energy sank into his eye socket, turning his brain to a hot pulp. He fell in perfect synchronization with the lowering of Adjutant Lux's plasma pistol back to his side. Lux then stood quietly again, like a statue, as if nothing had happened.

The other two racketeers peered down at their

dead companion and then at the weapon that lay beside him, tantalizingly close. Chodah remained fixed to the spot, while the other took a step closer to the rifle; as he did so, Lux brought the sidearm out in front of his stomach, deliberately displaying the weapon and his intent to use it again. The racketeer stopped. That the more junior of the two Hedalt soldiers had not already shot them suggested his intent was only to prevent them from recovering the weapons that lay strewn across the deck. The message was clear; to get past Adra they would have to fight her hand-to-hand.

Chodah had questioned Adra's bravery and this was a challenge not only to her honor, but to her capabilities as a fighter. Lux knew it was a challenge that could not go unanswered, and he was also eager to see the outcome. Adra was a skilled warrior, but two against one in any situation was always a risk, especially since racketeers were known for their ability to handle themselves.

There was silence as the two racketeers met each other's eyes, each realizing what they must do in order to survive. Together they drew blades from sheaths on their belts and advanced.

Chodah held back slightly and jolted to Adra's left, hoping to gain an advantage by allowing his more eager companion to draw her attack. There was a brief flurry of flashing metal and then the serrated edge of Adra's knife ripped through the racketeer's torso, sending a spray of his blood across Chodah's face. He smeared it clear of his eyes frantically and then lunged, sinking the tip of his blade into Adra's side, managing to slip it in-between the plates of armor. The Provost drew back, using the body of Chodah's companion as a shield. Still stunned from Adra's initial attack, the second racketeer desperately tried to break free of her grip, drawing his blade down across Adra's arm. She felt the sting of flesh being cut and the wetness of blood soaking into her clothing, before thrusting her serrated blade deep in the racketeer's gut, twisting it savagely and then ripping it back out like a saw cutting wood. The racketeer fell, clutching his opened stomach, while Chodah looked on with panicked eyes. Fearing the same fate, Chodah lashed out in a frenzy, but Adra dodged, avoiding the full force of the blow. Another trickle of blood trailed down Adra's thigh from the new cut, but she paid it no attention, and altered her stance, waiting for the perfect moment to attack. For a time they circled around each other, Chodah breathing heavily and blinking blood-smeared tears from his eyes, while Adra patiently measured her opponent, black blade dripping with red and poised with deadly intent. Eventually, Chodah's nerve failed and he lunged clumsily, allowing Adra to catch his wrist. Wasting no time, she twisted Chodah's arm back, opening up his body, before thrusting the onyx blade hilt-deep into his neck.

Lux had never witnessed a fight like this. It had been fast and brutal, with terrible injuries inflicted to all combatants. But it was the wide, bloodshot eyes of Chodah as Adra's knife ripped into his throat that surprised him the most. It was not a look of pain, but one of confusion; an inability to comprehend the sensation of the knife entering his flesh. But the confusion was short-lived as Adra withdrew the blade, coating her own face and neck with his blood, and allowed Chodah's body to fall alongside his dead crewmates; just another piece of discarded trash.

Lux holstered his weapon and waited as Adra cleaned her blade on the back of Chodah's jacket. She then returned it to a scabbard beneath her cloak and marched off the bridge of the racketeer ship, with Lux dutifully in tow. Adra had won her battle, but there was still another to fight.

TWENTY-EIGHT

Provost Adra monitored the approach of the newly-arrived racketeer ships, as they rapidly closed in on their position. Three simulants attended to her injuries as best they could, considering Adra was still wearing her armored uniform, which was now broken and bloodied like she was. Their ministrations had been sufficient to stem the bleeding from the most serious wounds, so that Adra was no longer at risk of bleeding to death. No-one walked away from a knife fight unscathed, and Adra knew that better than most, but her wounds would heal quickly. More importantly, there was no damage done to her reputation; if anything, the skirmish would only serve to enhance it.

Lux had not spoken a word to her about the

260

fight, and Adra knew that he would not bring it up. But, in time, when he was away from his posting or serving a new Provost, he would tell the story of how Adra fought and killed two racketeers on their own bridge, blade versus blade, thus ensuring that her reputation would only grow more fierce.

The bullet wound to Lux's thigh was also being attended to by a medical simulant. Though initially he had felt strangely little pain, his leg was now agonizing, and he was glad of his station at the front of the bridge, where no-one could see him grimace as the small metal slug was plucked from his flesh. Lux had been in battles before, but this had been the first time he'd been shot, by either a plasma shard or solid slug, and though he did not welcome the pain, he knew that Adra's mission log of the fight would indicate his injuries and the mettle he had shown when dealing with them.

"They will have closed to within weapons range in two minutes," said Lux, having deliberately waited for the pain meds to kick in a little before speaking, so that his voice would carry strongly to his commander. "Both are reading as Corvus-class cruisers; heavily modified."

Lux chose to say no more, since he presumed that Adra would also have studied the design of the approaching vessels. Then, as if on cue, one of the halo of screens above the command platform swung down on its metal arm and hung in front of the Provost. Less predictable was the matter of what his commander would do next. Adra knew as well as Lux did that two modified Corvus-class cruisers were a match even for their mighty War Frigate. It was one thing to fight two-on-one when each combatant had a blade, but battling two Corvus-class cruisers was akin to bringing a knife to a gunfight. Retreat was no dishonor in the face of impossible odds, but Provost Adra was one of the more obstinate Hedalt officers that he'd known. Retreat was not her style.

Adra finished studying the scan data of the approaching ships and moved the screen to her side, before brushing off the three medical simulants as if they were annoying, buzzy insects. Lux waited patiently, but with increasing anxiety, as the two Corvus-class cruisers closed to within a minute of firing range.

"Detach the racketeer vessel from our docking port and turn us away from the approaching ships," said Adra, grudgingly reaching the same conclusion as Lux without knowing it. "Prepare to jump to Way Station G-7J00; we will deal with these scum another day."

"Yes, Provost Adra," said Lux, at once both surprised by Adra's sensible decision and relieved by it. He had wondered if Adra choosing to withdraw would lessen his opinion of her, but it did not; only a fool would fight an unwinnable battle rather than risk losing face. He knocked the pilot simulant on the shoulder, and it immediately began turning the great frigate away from their pursuers. He then personally entered the jump parameters for Way Station G-7J00, plotting a direct reciprocal course. This would mean the computations would be swift enough that they could remain beyond the reach of the Corvus cruisers for long enough to jump clear.

Lux then poised his finger over the docking release, ready to discard the racketeer ship, now crewed only by corpses, from the underbelly of the frigate. But before he could execute the command, the bridge was rocked with a succession of powerful percussive thuds. Warnings flashed up on his console and on the viewport; the main engines lost power and consoles exploded all around the perimeter of the bridge, taking four simulant crew down with them. The lights dropped and the emergency lighting flickered on, bathing the bridge in a blood-red curtain of light, bleeding down from above.

"Mines..." Lux called back, realizing what had happened. "They must have attached gravity mines to the hull when we docked."

Adra jumped down from the command platform and rushed to Lux's side, reading the report on his screen. Lux observed her closely; if she was concerned, she did not show it. He hoped he did not show it either, though his insides felt like they'd turned to water. This wasn't a side-effect of the mines, but of worrying whether Adra would blame him for not detecting them.

The two cruisers were now within weapons range, but neither opened fire or sent any transmissions; they either intended to board or simply wanted to get close enough to make the kill feel personal.

Adra grabbed the primary pilot simulant by the arm and practically threw it out of the chair, before sliding down into the seat herself. "Go to the tactical station," Adra commanded, peering up at Lux. She spoke calmly, but her words flowed faster than usual and her brow shone with a light mist of sweat. "Divert all remaining power to the forward cannons. Take it from life support if you have to. And be ready; our survival depends on you."

A dozen questions flashed into Lux's mind, but there was no time to ask what Adra had planned, or exactly what she expected of him, and so instead he just ran to the tactical station, his legs almost collapsing from underneath him as the pain of his injury bit him again. He arrived to discover the main tactical console was damaged, but it still functioned well enough to do what Adra had commanded. A simulant lay on the deck, its artificial frame charred from the massive surge of energy that had discharged though its body, but

Lux just stepped over it and began to shunt all the power he could scavenge into the forward plasma cannons. The only system he could not bleed power from was the thruster controls which Adra had already pushed to double their capacity, using her command override to disable the safety protocols. *What are you going to do?* Lux asked silently, wracking his addled brain for a logical answer, but none came.

Suddenly, Lux felt as if a boot was pressing into his back and shoving him forward, and he had to grab the cool metal surround of the console to stop himself being squashed against it. Straining to maintain his position, he looked up at the viewport and saw that the ship was accelerating hard. He wrestled himself away from the console and noted that Adra had flipped the frigate so that its belly was aimed towards the racketeers, and that the dorsal thrusters were all firing simultaneously, burning so ferociously that they were on the verge of catastrophic failure. Suddenly, he understood Adra's plan. The most powerful weapon in their arsenal was not their plasma cannons, but the racketeer ship attached to their belly, and Adra intended to use it like a cannonball.

On the viewport, the two racketeer vessels began to veer away, as vibrations rippled through the bridge of the frigate. Adra checked the thruster controls and saw that almost half of the dorsal thrusters had already exploded, but the effect had only been to propel them even harder towards their enemy. With only seconds to impact, Adra hit the docking release and then shunted all power from the dorsal thrusters to the ventral thrusters, putting so much strain on the ship's hull that Adra heard the metal scream as it flexed. The frigate began to decelerate hard, while the small racketeer ship ploughed on towards the enemy vessels. Plasma energy tore through space as the lead racketeer cruiser fired its turrets towards the approaching projectile, but it only succeeded in turning its smaller comrade into a flaming warhead. A second later the ships collided and became one mass of fire, smoke and molten debris.

Provost Adra throttled back on the remaining thrusters, before they too exploded, and fought the nose of the War Frigate down as they rammed through what remained of the lead Corvus cruiser and Chodah's smaller vessel. But there was still the second cruiser to deal with, and as they emerged from the other side of the inferno, Lux realized what Adra had meant by 'our survival depends on you.' If he couldn't take it down, they were dead.

Though it had initially fled, the second Corvus was now bearing down on them. Plasma was unleashed from the weapon pods on its wing tips, but both shards flashed past, so close that Lux was sure he could feel their heat. But Lux was not afraid; the racketeer had taken its shot, and missed. Adra, still piloting the frigate on manual, angled the hawk-like craft towards their remaining enemy until the lethal forward cannons were aligned. Lux aimed and locked-on, taking over navigational control of the War Frigate in that crucial instant, and concentrated everything the mighty vessel had to offer into a single furious volley, so energetic that it melted and mangled the cannons, rendering them useless. But it did not matter, because Lux did not need to fire again. Ahead of them the Corvus-class cruiser sparked and hissed and spiraled out of control, split in two down the middle as if Lux had been a headsman that had wielded an enormous space axe.

Lux staggered back from the console and punched the air, shouting at the viewport in what was half victory cry, half war cry, the customary and expected stoicism of a Hedalt officer failing him. But Adra did not reprimand him this time. She simply pushed herself out of the pilot's chair, fists clenched and eyes burning hotter than the melted remains of their enemies. Unlike Lux, she found no pleasure in the victory, because the ship that Provost Adra wanted and hunted still evaded her. And the only other beings in the galaxy that had the ability to find them had all been vaporized into atoms.

TWENTY-NINE

Contingency One and the hauler emerged from the blind jump in perfect synchronization, with less than fifteen meters separating the belly of the hauler from the dorsal hull plating of the Corvette. In only a handful of maneuvers, Casey had become a master of the 'piggy back' as she had called it, hiding the hauler inside the transceiver envelope of the Contingency One. This had allowed both ships to jump along the threads of the Fabric, and past the Way Station without incident and without either ship registering on the CoreNet, thanks to the black market transceiver they'd acquired from the racketeer, Rheyda.

Despite the trouble the racketeers had caused them since, the transceiver had been pivotal in allowing them to rescue the engineers from the asteroid base. Now they were a solitary blind jump away from reaching the distant star system containing the main Contingency base. One jump from breathing new life into the centuries-old plan to fight back against the Hedalt and re-take Earth.

"We're going to need to transfer some fuel to the hauler for the last jump, Cap," said Casey, spinning around in the pilot's chair. "Sorry, I mean Commander S; force of habit!"

"Get out of that habit, pilot," Sonner replied from the command chair, with her characteristic charm. It was a friendly kind of snarkiness that Casey had begun to recognize as merely an element of Sonner's prickly, but likeable personality. And in the same way that she'd learnt to recognize when to and when not to push Taylor's buttons, she was also becoming adept at manipulating Sonner. It helped that Casey's genius piloting had already saved their skins – organic and synthetic – multiple times, and combined with her effervescent personality, which was like a fizzing tonic to a bad hangover, it was hard to stay mad at Casey, or even get mad at her in the first place.

"Aye aye, Commander Sarah Sonner," replied Casey as the chair spun around twice more. "It will take a couple of hours to make the transfer; handy to have a bunch of engineers around!"

"Yes it is," said Sonner, with a sense of pride.

"Everyone take a well-earned break in that case; we'll reconvene in ninety minutes." Then she pushed herself out of the chair and almost fell over.

"Woah there, Commander, take it easy..." said Taylor, who had been standing close by and instinctively went to catch her, but Sonner waved him off. Taylor stood back, but continued to watch over her attentively. "When was the last time you slept?"

"For more than a couple of hours? Hell knows," grunted Sonner, "I'll sleep when we're docked back at the Contingency base and no sooner," she added, turning towards the exit, shoulders slouchy and feet dragging on the deck. "Now, if you'll excuse me, I have a date with three or four more strong black coffees, which should hopefully stop me falling on my face."

Taylor stroked his chin, still expecting to feel stubble and still being surprised by its absence, "I guess I'll get some rest too then," he said, realizing that once they entered the lava tube again his connection to the CoreNet would be cut off, along with his ability to potentially speak to Satomi. And despite the unsettling experience he'd had the last time he tried to reach her, and the strange sense of foreboding he still felt because of her warning to him, he didn't want to waste the opportunity. If he was ever to find her, he needed Satomi to show him where she was. He glanced back at Casey, who was spinning around in her chair again, flashing her red sneakers. "Remember that you need to rest too, Casey. Or, your brain does at least."

"I know, Cap, I'll do it later, I promise," Casey replied, her voice rising and lowering in volume as she continued to spin around in the pilot's chair. "Commander S has sorted out my quarters. I can't go bouncing around inside the Fabric like you do, though."

Taylor walked up beside her and rested against the console, "What do you do then?" he asked, genuinely interested in what Casey saw while 'sleeping'.

Casey stopped spinning and rested her feet on the console next to Taylor. "Mostly, I just like to lie back and look at the stars. It's peaceful; probably the most at peace I've ever felt, or remember feeling. It's hard to know what's real."

Taylor nodded, "I know what you mean. I'm still trying to get my head around it too."

"Sometimes, I look back into her memories," Casey continued, her expression turning studious and pokerfaced, which made her look like a different person. "You know, the original Casey?" she added, rhetorically. "At least, I think they're her memories. It doesn't really feel like me, you know? Like you're watching someone else's home movie, except the people in the pictures just happen to look like you."

Taylor remembered seeing his apartment by the Columbia River, and even seeing Casey sitting at the table on the balcony, and he knew exactly what Casey meant. He still didn't know if that place had really existed, or if he'd know the original Casey three hundred years earlier. "I guess we just have to make some new memories," Taylor answered, "Some real memories of our real lives."

Casey's expression seemed to harden and she began to rub the back of her hand with her thumb, something Taylor had never seen her do before. But as he often needed to remind himself this was a unique Casey Valera, not the Casey he knew or remembered.

"Do you think we can pull this off?" she asked, hesitantly, as if asking the question was forbidden. "Even if we find crews for this fleet of Nimrods Commander S is hiding, we're fighting an armada three centuries more advanced, with probably a fraction of the numbers."

Taylor considered a white lie; telling Casey that he believed the Contingency could work, even though in reality he had no idea if it had any chance of success, and even shared Casey's doubts. But there had been enough lies. "Honestly, Casey, I have no idea," he answered, and Casey's eyes dropped low, staring at the thumb that was rubbing her hand harder and faster. "But I do know this; we have to try. Win or lose, we can't just give in and slink off to some unexplored part of the galaxy to hide."

"Why not?" asked Casey, "The galaxy is a big place. We could go somewhere the Hedalt would never find us, and start again. If we fight, we risk losing everything, for good this time."

"There is that risk," Taylor agreed. "But what if we could kick the Hedalt off Earth? What if we could take it back?"

Casey considered this for a moment, "It was never ours to lose, Cap," she said, sadly. "It was never our home. Not really."

"I know, I think about that a lot too," admitted Taylor, "but after what they did to us, it would feel good to get some payback, and I can't think of a better way."

Casey snorted a laugh, "I don't think I'm the hero type, Cap."

"Be not afraid of greatness..." Taylor began, annunciating in his best theatrical accent.

Casey laughed more heartily this time, "Please, Cap, no more Shakespeare." Then she glanced over at the tactical console. "Besides, it's not as much fun without Blake to pluck Satomi's strings."

"We'll find him too, Casey," said Taylor, resting a hand on her shoulder, "We'll find them both."

"So we save Earth and put the crew back together!" said Casey, speaking like a movie trailer voice-over, before adding, hopefully, "And then what?"

This time Taylor shrugged, "Then we'll see what the galaxy has in store for us next." He pushed away from the console and began to briskly pace towards the exit, "Now, if you don't mind, my squishy human brain is going to get some rest."

"Night night, Captain Taylor Ray," Casey called back, waving a hand. Then she waited until the door slid open and thudded shut again, before adding, under her breath, despite the bridge being empty save for her, "If you find her out there in the Fabric, tell her I said hi."

THIRTY

Taylor stepped through the starlight door and sat down on the translucent floor of the corridor that extended into space without end. He gazed out at the surrounding blanket of stars and the array of wire-framed cubes that each marked the location of a super-luminal transceiver. She was out there somewhere, close to one of the countless glowing cubes. He just had to find her.

He closed his eyes and turned his mind to thoughts of Satomi Rose, as if trying to dial her number in the great cosmic cell phone network that he was somehow able to tap into. But, as often happened when he wanted to remember Satomi's face, he was unable to recall her likeness. He cursed and opened his eyes again. The irony was that her image would often leap into his mind at random, usually inopportune moments, when he needed to focus on something important. Then, her face would crystallize as clearly as if she was standing in front of him. When he wanted to remember, as he did then, he was often left with a faceless shadow.

Casey had been right about the tranquility of this strange corridor in space that they could both now inhabit, even though she was unable to venture through the starlight door into the Fabric. The stillness was relaxing, almost meditative. From his memory of the original Taylor Ray, he had not been a spiritual person, and he didn't consider himself to be either, but there was something about this place that was almost ethereal. It was a sanctuary only for the mind, and perhaps the place where he was still the most human.

"Taylor, are you there?" came a voice, at first distant and then clearer. It was Satomi. Taylor sprang back to his feet and peered along the invisible corridor, half-expecting to find her standing in front of him, but there was only darkness, punctuated by pin-pricks of starlight.

"Yes, I can hear you," Taylor answered into the emptiness, with the excitement of a child, "But I don't have long. Do you remember what I told you, the last time we spoke?"

"Yes, vaguely, but it seems so long ago," said

Satomi, sounding weary. "I remember being somewhere else, and I remember warning you about something, but it's hazy, like a half-remembered dream, or more like a nightmare. It used to be that I could barely remember this strange starlit emptiness, but now it's more real to me than anything else. Is it really true. Am I really not human?"

"Can you tell me where you are? Where your body is, not where your mind is?" said Taylor, focusing on the sound of her voice. He didn't want to be distracted by talk of who or what she was; what mattered was where she was. And then suddenly he was moving through the Fabric, flying along the threads at impossible speeds. He closed his eyes to blot out the dizzying blur of stars and called out, "Show me where you are, when you're not here with me. Picture it in your mind and describe it to me; I'll come for you."

"All I know is that it's not a ship," said Satomi, "It's foggy, but the more I talk to you, the clearer things become." Then she picked up on what Taylor had said. "What do you mean you'll come for me? How?"

"I'll come for you and break you free," said Taylor, rushing through another node. "We have a ship. I already found Casey; I mean another simulant version of Casey Valera. She's like me now. She's alive, Satomi, and you can be too, free from the Hedalt!"

"Am I not alive now?" asked Satomi, sounding confused, as if dosed up on painkillers. "If I'm not alive, then what am I?"

"You're Satomi Rose," said Taylor, breaking through another node, but he was slowing down now, as if there was a rope tied to his waist, pulling him back. There was a dull ache building at the back of his head, but he ignored it and opened his eyes to see a gloomy, grey planet and a strange, almost metallic-looking moon, lit by a vivid yellow star. "I think I'm close, hold on, Satomi..."

But then Taylor felt the stabbing pain inside his head begin to grow. *No, not yet, let me see her!* Taylor screamed inside his mind, but it was no use; he was yanked away and the planet vanished. He screamed, but the stars again became a blur, as he rushed back along a different thread of the Fabric, like a fish caught on a line and being reeled in by an eager angler. "Satomi!" he bellowed, "Satomi, can you hear me?!" but there was no answer. Taylor was spiraling, faster and further, bouncing from one node to another, and becoming lost in the Fabric. His eyes darkened and his mind was in a spin as the acceleration became overwhelming; he tried to scream again, but no sound came out of his mouth. Then there was darkness and a dizzying silence, but he was still conscious. Disembodied and cut-off from everything but his own thoughts,

Taylor was still alive; though where he was he did not know. Slowly, his vision began to return and he heard voices, muffled at first but steadily growing louder and clearer.

"The CoreNet signal anomaly has grown in intensity, Provost," said a male voice, "it seems to have been drawn here when we focused in on the signal. Shall I initiate the purge?"

"No, not yet," said a female voice. A strong, confident voice. "Monitor the anomaly and stand ready with the signal purge. I want to see what it does."

"Yes, Provost Adra," said the male, drumming commands into his console at the front of the bridge. "It now appears to be stable, but the intensity has increased dramatically."

His senses cleared and Taylor found himself lying on the bridge of a Hedalt warship; the same bridge he had seen in a previous jaunt through the Fabric. He stood up, but though he appeared to be on the deck, his feet did not touch metal. It was the same sensation as being inside the deep space corridor.

Taylor could see two Hedalt soldiers, dressed in the same armored black uniform that Sonner had adopted as a disguise, except these soldiers looked like they had just fought a war. Their backs were facing him, but he could still make out that their clothes were bloodied and torn. The bridge itself was also damaged, with some consoles still smoldering and sparking. There were simulant bodies littering the deck too, each with plasticine, anonymous faces and grim, soulless expressions that looked no more alive than those of their still functional counterparts, a dozen of which bustled around the bridge. Then the soldiers turned and Taylor felt a sudden coldness as he recognized them as the same two officers he had seen before.

Adra turned around, eyes scrunched into a scowl, as if she had heard an intruder breaking in. "Exactly how localized is this anomaly, Adjutant Lux?" she said, as if sensing Taylor's presence. Taylor took a step back, unnerved by the soldier's reaction.

"I cannot determine a precise position," Lux replied after a few moments. "But, curiously, I am also reading a flux in our transceiver and super-luminal engines; both are consistent with the residual energy signature of a jump."

Adra stepped into the center of the command platform and remained deathly still and silent, eyes flicking around the bridge. "I believe it is here."

Lux turned and peered at her, "The Hunter simulant, here, now? But how is that possible?"

Adra did not answer her Adjutant's question; instead, her sharp blue eyes remained focused ahead, as if she was staring directly at Taylor. He remained perfectly still. *Surely, she cannot see me?* He thought.

Lux drew his sidearm and began to scan his eyes all around the bridge anxiously. Then he felt anger at the absurdity of his reaction – what use was a weapon against a signal inside the CoreNet? – and quickly lowered it to his side, hiding it inside his long cloak, and hoping that Adra had not seen his actions, and judged him on them.

"If you can hear me, know this," announced Adra, addressing the bridge as if it were an amphitheater. "I will find you and the human you harbor. I don't care what you think you are. You were made in a laboratory, by my own hand. You are not human, though you are equally as worthless as them to me. You are just a simulant, a malfunctioning slave of the empire, and I will hunt you down and destroy you all."

Taylor was enraged, and to his surprise he actually felt it – truly felt it – as if he once again had blood coursing through veins. He may only have existed as energy inside the Fabric, but the visceral state of fury he was experiencing was no different to a human body that had flooded with a volatile cocktail of endorphins, adrenaline and dopamine. And he wanted to use this anger; use it against the monster that stood in front of him. The one that had twisted him into a weapon and that threatened again to destroy the people he cared about. His family.

Taylor marched towards Adra, raising his fist with the intention to strike her, not knowing if that was even possible, but as he advanced he brushed past an idling simulant and was drawn to it, like iron filings to a magnet. His fist clung to the simulant's arm, but instead of feeling nothing, the contact with the simulant was like an electrical charge. He tried to pull his fist back and then, without thinking, placed his other hand on the simulant's body to help press himself away. But instead of breaking free, Taylor was absorbed into the simulant's body like a sponge drawing in water. There was a flash of light and a feeling like being struck by lightning, but then these sensations were gone and Taylor found himself seeing the bridge as if viewed through the simulant's eyes. He was no longer an ethereal spectator, but physically in the presence of the military Provost who had threatened him.

Adra was transfixed by the sudden and bizarre behavior of the simulant, which twitched and spasmed feverishly, as if being struck with a dozen cattle prods. Lux's reaction had been more wary; he did not share his commander's curiosity and had moved swiftly to take up position just behind her, his weapon still poised and ready inside his coat.

Taylor briefly caught sight of the plasma pistol

beneath Lux's billowing coat and panicked. His first thought was to rush at the Provost and use her as a shield, but he soon realized he was powerless to do anything; he had no control over the simulant body he had somehow possessed. His rational mind reasserted itself. *I'm not really here...* He told himself... *Do nothing; they can't kill a ghost...* But he did not want to do nothing; rage still bubbled inside him. He knew Sonner would have told him to stop, and not do anything that might confirm their suspicions, but it was clear to Taylor that this Provost Adra had already caught their scent. She was coming for them no matter what.

"You tried to destroy us once before and failed, Provost Adra," said Taylor, giving in to his anger. To his surprise the simulant spoke his words, but with a clinicality that was even more sinister and threatening than he'd intended. "You failed then. You will fail again."

Adra stepped towards to the simulant, with Lux following close behind and raising the previously concealed weapon towards it.

"So, it is true," said Adra, sounding almost pleased with herself. "Some humans did survive, and now they are using my simulants as pets." She took another step closer to the haunted automaton and peered into its silver eyes with pure hatred and contempt. It felt to Taylor like she was staring straight into his soul. "Do you really think you have a chance? A simulant, created from the brain of one of four uniquely fallible and susceptible humans, each one gullible enough to believe the fantasy I created for them?" She laughed in the simulant's face. "You're more the enemy of the humans than we are." Then she cocked her head and held her chin gently with thumb and forefinger. "If I were to guess, I'd say you were the pathetically romantic Satomi Rose simulant, or perhaps the idealistic imbecile, Captain Taylor Ray?"

"Nice try, Provost, but you'll get nothing from me," said Taylor, fighting the urge to explode at her again, but he could hear Sonner's voice in his head, telling him to not be so damn stupid... "Nothing except the knowledge that I'm out here, and that I'm not alone. But you already knew that much, didn't you?"

"I know more than your inferior human brain could ever comprehend," Adra spat.

"Well, comprehend this," said Taylor, willing the simulant body to move so he could grab Adra by the throat, but still it would not budge, "Your little vacation on Earth is coming to an end. I'd leave, while you still have the chance."

Adra laughed again, but this was a freer laugh, rather than one borne from cruelty; it was a reaction that neither Taylor nor – judging from the ashen look on his face – Lux had anticipated. "Your human friends have no claim on Earth, and you even less so. Earth had always belonged to the Hedaltus race. It is ours by right, and we shall never forsake it." Then she stripped the plasma pistol from Lux's hand and stepped directly in front of the simulant, towering over the manufactured body. Then with her voice no louder than a whisper, yet still possessing a power that could have cracked steel, she said, "Tell your friends I am coming for them." She raised the weapon, pressed the barrel to the simulant's head and fired.

The simulant body crumpled to the deck, its cranial unit split and melting and sparking into flames. Adra handed the pistol back to Lux and stepped back onto the command platform, as if nothing had happened. "Continue to monitor the CoreNet for anomalies," she ordered, with an almost eerie calmness that was at odds with the torrent of emotions flooding through Lux's body.

Lux rushed back to his console and quickly updated the scans. The anomaly had gone, but a residual signal was still detected, travelling away from the ship at super-luminal speeds back along one of the billions of threads of the Fabric, but still impossible to trace. He turned back to Adra, filled with excitement and fear and nervous energy, "Perhaps you destroyed it, Provost?"

"No..." said Adra, without hesitation or doubt,

"it is still out there, as is the human pestilence it now serves." Then she looked up at the circle of screens above her, checking on the progress of the probes that were still scouring the asteroid field. "Buried within this system the humans have hidden something," she said, talking more to herself than to Lux. "And when we find it, we will be one step closer to finding them. And then I will wipe out the last remains of humanity, once and forever."

THIRTY-ONE

The bridge door slid open and Taylor stepped through, grabbing onto the frame for support as it thudded into the housing. It had been a full twenty minutes since his experience on the Hedalt warship, and while the military Provost hadn't actually shot him in the head with a plasma pistol, it certainly felt like she had. It was like someone had removed his brain and played basketball with it for a few minutes, before slam-dunking it back inside his head. Mercifully, the pain had only lasted until he had passed through the starlight door and regained consciousness in his quarters, but while his head no longer hurt, since his simulant body felt no pain, the delirious effects had yet to fully wear off. It was like being drunk without the humorous benefits.

"Finally, there you are," snapped Sonner, glancing back as Taylor stepped onto the bridge. On the main viewport he could see they were already approaching the mouth of the narrow cave that lead into the lava tube where the Contingency base resided, shielded from the galactic reach of the Fabric and CoreNet. "I've been buzzing your quarters for the last ten minutes. Where the hell have you been?"

"Sorry, I guess I overslept," said Taylor, standing just behind the command chair and resting an elbow on it for support. He didn't want to get into a discussion with Sonner about what had happened; at least, not yet.

Sonner glanced up at him again, "Rough night, Captain? You look like I feel every morning."

"You could say that," Taylor replied, "I'll fill you in later, Commander."

Sonner cocked an eyebrow at Taylor and then studied his smooth face and silver eyes for a few seconds, before turning back to the viewport, "Fair enough, Captain, but I'll hold you to it. No secrets, remember?"

"I remember, Commander, but trust me, now is not the time."

"You might want to take a seat, Cap," Casey called out from the pilot's console; she was peering into her dedicated viewport and controlling the Contingency One on full manual, with the hauler tethered to her every movement. "You're about to witness me become the first pilot to successfully navigate a lava tube in a cruiser-class ship."

Taylor made his way over to the tactical station, staggering every third step, and dropped down into the seat. "Actually, you're not the first to do this," he said, knowing that his original Casey actually held that honor. But since the Casey sitting in the pilot's chair was ostensibly the same person, technically she was still correct. "Well, I mean you sort of are, but then it wasn't really you either. Even though it was." Sonner and Casey both looked at him like he'd gone mad.

"You alright, Cap?" said Casey, in a way that suggested she thought he wasn't. "Did you hit your cranial unit or something?" she added, with a smirk.

"I'm fine, it's just... complicated."

"How about you two save this little chit-chat until after we've navigated several hundred tons of space cruisers containing all that remains of humanity though a narrow rocky tunnel?" said Sonner, layering on the sarcasm thickly.

"Aye aye, Commander Sarah Sonner" replied Casey and Taylor in unison. They looked at each other and burst out laughing, but their slightly artificial sounding mirth wasn't shared by Sonner, who rested her head in her hands and shook it gently.

"Honestly, we may as well surrender to the Hedalt now," said Sonner, only half-joking.

"Aww, don't be like that Commander S," said Casey, focusing her attention back into the pilot's viewport. Then Casey's demeanor shifted, as if someone had flipped a switch in her head, and her concentration became razor-sharp. "Entering the tunnel... now. All readings looking good and the hauler is tight in behind."

A silence fell over the bridge as Taylor and Sonner both understood the importance of this moment in time, and neither wanted to interrupt Casey during such a critical period. Alarms periodically sounded on the bridge and both Taylor and Sonner silently and anxiously peered down at their panels and consoles, noting the distance to collision indicators rising and falling, dropping to only two meters at one point, before eventually they all fell silent and both ships emerged through the other side of the tunnel and into the vast lava tube.

"Hauler One, you now have control," said Casey into the communicator, before relinquishing her telemetric grip over the other ship and pumping up the forward floodlights to maximum. The hauler did the same a moment later, but even together they were unable to illuminate the vast cavern fully.

Sonner tapped a command into her pad, "Casey,

I've just sent you the hangar co-ordinates and docking access," she said. "Tell the hauler to follow you in."

Casey replied with her customary acceptance and relayed the co-ordinates, before adjusting course and taking the Corvette lower, back towards the command center and trio of hangars where Taylor's new life had begun. He looked at Casey and smiled; seeing her in the pilot's seat again felt good. But then his smile faded away, remembering how she and Blake and Satomi – his original crew – had all fallen in the place where he was again headed. That this Casey was so like the one he knew made it easier to cope with – so easy that it was like she had never really died – but at the same time he felt guilt at how quickly he'd moved on. Once again, he was glad of how his simulant body was unable to reproduce the sickening sensation he would otherwise be feeling.

The outer doors to the giant hangar bay slid back and Casey maneuvered the Contingency One inside, followed slowly and considerably more cautiously by the bulkier hauler. The airlock re-pressurized and the inner door opened, revealing the row of pristine Nimrod-class cruisers that sat still and silent, like a space-age Terracotta Army, waiting to be reawakened from their centuries-long slumber and pressed into battle.

"Home sweet home," said Casey, flipping

switches in an elaborate ballet of movements to power down the engines and engage the parking systems. "Not that I've ever seen this place before, of course."

"It's a damn sight better than that cesspit of a Way Station we picked you up in, that's for sure," said Taylor. Then he checked the external sensors and saw that the engineering crew were already disembarking from the hauler. "You'd better get out there, Commander. Your subjects await..."

Sonner sprang up out of the command chair, "You're coming too, Captain. After all, you're the second most senior Earth Fleet officer left."

"I doubt they're going to want to take orders from a simulant," said Taylor, pushing himself out of the chair with far less enthusiasm than Sonner had done.

"We're all going to have to get used to things being different, Captain," said Sonner, with a brightness that almost matched Casey's default level of exuberance. "But when you and I left this base, we were one human and one simulant and one ship against the combined might of the Hedalt Empire." She pressed a button on the panel in the command chair and a view of the engineers filing out of the hauler and lining up, under the command of Sarah Sonner's younger brother appeared on the viewport. "Now look at how far we've come," she added, gesturing to the screen as if it was a canvas containing a masterpiece that she'd been working on for a decade. "We have ships, we have engineers, and we have the best damn pilot in the galaxy..." Casey gave a flourish and a little bow, "Now we only need flight crews and the Contingency is reborn!"

Taylor smiled. He admired Sonner's optimism, especially for someone so often grouchy, and he couldn't deny that what they had already achieved was remarkable. He glanced over to Casey and she was smiling too. "Okay, Commander, let's go and meet the troops."

"Engineers..." Sonner corrected, proudly, before turning and breezing off the bridge as if she was walking on a cloud.

Taylor and Casey followed her off the bridge and down the rear cargo ramp onto the hangar deck, but hung back to let Sonner enjoy her moment. At least the crew massing on the deck outside already knew the fate of their world, and the reason they were out here, and it showed in how easily they appeared to adapt to their new environment. Taylor envied them this; to him, the Contingency base still seemed strange and alien, and only his ship felt like somewhere he truly belonged.

"Whatcha thinkin', Cap?" said Casey, and Taylor realized she'd been watching him out of the corner of her silver eye.

Taylor sighed, "I'm not sure," he confessed, "I guess I just don't feel like I fit in here. It was different when it was just me and Sonner..." Casey coughed elaborately, "and you, of course..." Taylor added, smiling, "but now it just seems like we're spectators."

"I know what you mean," said Casey, resting an arm on his shoulder, "None of this really belongs to us, does it? This base, the Contingency, Earth, any of it. We're just hitchhikers along for the ride."

Taylor was surprised how comfortably Casey had accepted this, and how freely she had admitted it. "And that doesn't bother you?"

Casey shrugged, "I only ever wanted to fly, Cap," she said, with a softness that he rarely heard from her. "When I'm flying, I'm home. Perhaps once we stop the Hedalt, we'll both be free to fly wherever we like."

Taylor smiled, "I wish I was so certain about my future," he said, envious of Casey's clarity.

"You'll figure it out Cap," said Casey, slapping him on the back. "Now, I'm going to take a look around one of those shiny new Nimrods!"

Taylor laughed and watched Casey run up to the closest of the Nimrod-class cruisers sitting on the deck, and run her hand along the front docking strut, as if she was stroking a beloved pet. Then he looked over at the new crew of engineers, already bustling with energy and purpose, working under the command of the two Sonner siblings. Already there was a hum in the air as power was restored to parts of the hangar that had been dormant for more than three hundred years. Sonner was right, the Contingency was coming to life. Then he thought again about Satomi and what he would do or say if he ever did find her again. But that was for another time, he realized; a time when the Hedalt were confronted and defeated. There was no escaping that now; not after his encounter with Provost Adra. Even after three centuries, they had not forgotten and they would never stop hunting them.

Taylor stepped back up the ramp of the Contingency One, the Hedalt Corvette that was the closest thing to home that Taylor had, and headed for the bridge. There was a serenity about the ship now; with most of its systems powered down, and no-one else on-board, it should have felt lonely, but it didn't. To Taylor, it felt comforting, like a hot drink on a cold night. He dropped into the command chair, removed the data pad stowed in the arm, and logged into the account, 'Taylor Ray - Awake'.

THIRTY-TWO

Personal Journal - Entry #2
  I can hardly believe this is only my second journal entry since I was awakened and began my new life. My only life. So much has happened already, I don't know where to begin. The human engineer who was my enemy is now my friend, and my commanding officer. She has more prickles than a damn hedgehog and is one of the snarkiest, grumpiest Earth Fleet officers I've ever met, or at least have a memory of meeting. But she also engenders trust in a way I never thought possible, and she has heart. Not the organic, beating kind, though she has one of those too, but the kind that means you care more deeply than most other people do. I might not have a real heart anymore, but I hope I still care even half as much

as she does.

And then there's Casey Valera. She might not be the Casey I knew, but she's every bit the Casey I remember, and so much more. She's already saved our skins more than once, and with any luck, she can help me find Blake and Satomi too. I know that my needs are nothing when weighed against the survival of the human race and the rescue of Earth, but Casey, Blake and Satomi are my family, and they're all I have.

Perhaps the biggest surprise of all is that the Contingency has come to life, and as impossible as it sounds, maybe we do have a chance. We've already beaten the odds more times that I care to count and we can beat them again. We have to. We no longer have a choice. The Hedalt know we're out here and they're looking for us, and I know, one way or another, we'll have to fight.

Do I know yet who I am? No, but I'm learning fast. I know I'm brave – maybe even a little stupid – and I know that family means more to me than the Earth itself. Hopefully, I can have both. I also know the face of my enemy, and I've looked into her eyes. Through them I've seen the hatred and cruelty of the Hedalt Empire, and its resolve to wipe us out for good. They believe Earth is theirs by right. Why, I don't know, but I know they won't give it up easily. They will fight for Earth, just as hard as the humans will. Just as hard as I will. I should be afraid of what's coming, but I'm not. Let Provost Adra come. Let them all come. We'll be ready for them. The Contingency War has begun.

The end.

TO BE CONTINUED...

The Contingency War series continues in book three, *Rise of Nimrod Fleet*.

Rise of Nimrod Fleet:

All the books in the series:

- The Contingency
- The Waystation Gambit
- Rise of Nimrod Fleet
- Earth's Last War

ALSO BY THIS AUTHOR

If you enjoyed this book, please consider reading The Planetsider Trilogy, also by G J Ogden. Available from Amazon and free to read for Kindle Unlimited subscribers.

The Planetsider Trilogy:
A post-apocalyptic thriller with a military Sci-Fi twist

- The Planetsider

- The Second Fall

- The Last of the Firsts

*"The strong action sequences and thoughtful worldbuilding make this one worth picking up for fans of plot-driven SF." - **Publishers Weekly***

ABOUT THE AUTHOR

At school I was asked to write down the jobs I wanted to do as a 'grown up'. Number one was astronaut and number two was a PC games journalist. I only managed to achieve one of those goals (I'll let you guess which), but these two very different career options still neatly sum up my lifelong interests in science, space and the unknown.

School also steered me in the direction of a science-focused education over literature and writing, which influenced my decision to study physics at Manchester University. What this degree taught me is that I didn't like studying physics and instead enjoyed writing, which is why you're reading this book! The lesson? School can't tell you who you are.

When not writing, I enjoy spending time with my family, walking in the British countryside, and indulging in as much Sci-Fi as possible.

You can connect with me here:
https://twitter.com/GJ_Ogden
https://www.facebook.com/PlanetsiderNovel

Subscribe to my newsletter:
http://subscribe.ogdenmedia.net

Made in the USA
Monee, IL
30 March 2022